The further they traveled into the city, the more impassable the roads became. Lady A had to slow their vehicle practically to a crawl to avoid rubble strewn across the street, and sometimes had to backtrack and take an alternate route when the road ahead was completely blocked. None of them wanted to get out of the car and investigate the ruins on foot; the stench was too noxious, and it was already abundantly clear how thorough the invaders' bombardment had been. Any planet falling to their attack would suffer horrible casualties.

They rode mostly in silence, both out of respect for the dead and in awe of the enemy's power. One unanswered question hung heavily in their minds: *Where were the invaders?*

By the same author

The *Lensman* Series

*Triplanetary*
*First Lensman*
*Second Stage Lensmen*
*Grey Lensman*
*Galactic Patrol*
*Children of the Lens*
*Masters of the Vortex*

The *Skylark* Series

*The Skylark of Space*
*Skylark Three*
*Skylark of Valeron*
*Skylark DuQuesne*

The *Family d'Alembert* Series (with Stephen Goldin)

*The Imperial Stars*
*Stranglers' Moon*
*The Clockwork Traitor*
*The Bloodstar Conspiracy*
*Getaway World*
*The Purity Plot*
*Planet of Treachery*
*Eclipsing Binaries*

Other Novels

*Spacehounds of IPC*
*The Galaxy Primes*
*Subspace Explorers*
*Subspace Encounter*

E. E. 'DOC' SMITH
WITH STEPHEN GOLDIN

# The Omicron Invasion

Volume 9 in *The Family d'Alembert* Series

PANTHER
Granada Publishing

Panther Books
Granada Publishing Ltd
8 Grafton Street, London W1X 3LA

First published in Great Britain by Panther Books 1984

Copyright © Verna Smith Trestrail 1984

ISBN 0-586-04342-X

Printed and bound in Great Britain by
Collins, Glasgow

Set in Times

Dedicated to the Los Angeles Science Fantasy Society, Inc. and, in particular, to Alexis Walser and Alan Trimpi – for sharing their space for a while

– S.G.

# CHAPTER 1

## *Omicron*

With nearly fourteen hundred planets in the Empire of Earth, each world either had to strive to attain its own distinct character or end up as an anonymous statistic in galactic society. Some worlds, by their physical nature, had it easier than others; they could claim to be hotter or colder, wetter or drier, bigger or smaller than other planets. They could have unusual configurations of moons, heavier or lighter gravity, variable or multiple suns, or even be surrounded by ring systems of moonlets. They could become noted for some strange native plant or animal, or for some natural resource or bizarre topographical feature. Such worlds had their reputations already established; you merely had to mention their names and even schoolchildren could tell you something about them. Names like DesPlaines, Gastonia, or Floreata conjured instant images in people's minds.

Other worlds were noted more for their cultures than for their physical attributes. During the great exodus from Earth in the twenty-first century, many separate cultures were established so their inhabitants could be free to pursue the lifestyles they preferred. Some planets were settled by religious fanatics; Purity became a haven for hardline Judaeo-Christian fundamentalists, Anares was settled by Oriental mystics, and Delf – well, no one from outside the planet ever had a clear idea *what* the Delfians believed in, but they were quiet about their faith and seldom bothered others, so they were tolerated in the cosmopolitan imperial society.

Still other worlds established their character only after

settlement. The inhabited moon Vesa became an empire-wide tourist attraction because of its exotic gambling parlors; Glasseye became the symbol of transience and impermanence because of its inhabitants' fascination with newness. Becoming different or unique was a way of establishing a reputation.

The planet Omicron was undistinguished as far as physical appearance and climate were concerned. It came close to being a twin of Earth, circling a yellow star and having but one large moon. The polar caps were suitably cold, the equatorial zone was suitably hot; there were deserts and rainforests, mountains and plains, oceans and continents. The native lifeforms were distinctive – as were the lifeforms on every planet – but none were so unusual they'd instantly bring the name Omicron to mind. The people who had settled Omicron in the late 2300s were decent, hardworking folk from a variety of social and religious backgrounds – hardly the fanatical types needed to create a public relations image. By the reign of Empress Stanley Eleven the planetary population was approaching a hundred million – a drop in the bucket compared to Earth and other population centers, but still bigger than many other worlds.

Omicron's sole claim to fame was distance. At nine hundred and sixty-nine parsecs from Earth, it was easily the most distant planet ever settled. Located at the outer rim of Sector Twelve, it represented humanity's deepest penetration into the heart of the Milky Way Galaxy. Omicron stood at the Empire's edge, far removed from the bustle and furor of imperial civilization. The name Omicron conjured visions of incalculable distance, as the phrase 'the ends of the Earth' had done in earlier times.

Because it was so far away from the center of activity, Omicron was often a little behind the times. Imperial fashions tended to reach it later, and gossip was usually wildly distorted by the time it reached the outpost of civilization. The people of Omicron didn't mind; they were largely self-sufficient, and viewed their separation from the mainstream of interstellar society as a form of independence. One local wag had called Omicron 'the wart on the end of the Empire's nose,' and the citizens had adopted that epithet with a perverse enjoyment.

In 2451, Empress Stanley Eleven was well past the second anniversary of her coronation, and peace had returned to the Empire once more. The horror of the Coronation Day Incursion, that ruthless attack upon Earth, was but an unpleasant memory in the minds of most people. The common man still could not understand the precise circumstances that brought the raid about, nor did he know who the Empress's enemies were. The palace had issued reassuring pronouncements, though, and the subsequent years of tranquility had calmed the populace.

Only the upper echelons of imperial government remained concerned, because they alone knew that the threat was far from over. The vast hidden conspiracy had made one direct assault against the Service of the Empire six months after the coronation; when that failed, it was followed by an ominous silence that made everyone more than a little nervous. A silent enemy is the worst of all.

None of these matters really bothered the citizens of Omicron. They were so far away from the center of any action that it was hard for them to care. The wise and just reigns of Stanley Ten and Eleven had numbed them to political reality. What did it matter who was on the Throne, they thought; Earth was so far away that the administration had little impact on their daily lives.

Then one horrifying day, death rained out of the skies. Nonnuclear bombs began falling on the major cities and settlements of Omicron simultaneously all over the planet. There was never any accurate count of the people killed and wounded in those first few minutes, but the number easily ran into the millions. People died as buildings collapsed around them; others died from flying debris or the concussions of explosions. The SOTE office in Omicron City, the planet's capital, was smashed to rubble. Between one moment and the next, devastation and disaster settled upon peaceful Omicron.

Because Omicron was the planet farthest from the imperial center, the Navy had a base located there. Several battleships and cruisers were stationed at the Omicron base, and it had always been considered a quiet assignment; aside from occasional maneuvers and war games, nothing ever happened. Even pirates and smugglers left Omicron alone; perhaps they felt it would not be worth their while to travel so far for the small potential rewards.

The Navy must have been as surprised as everyone else by the suddenness of the attack. There must have been someone manning the sensor screens when the invading ships appeared out of subspace. An alarm of some sort must have been given. The Navy crews must have scrambled frantically into their ships even as a challenge was broadcast to the unknown force overhead, either to identify themselves or to leave the vicinity of the planet immediately.

As well trained as the Imperial Navy was, it would be difficult to believe they would not have responded instantly to the threat. But standard procedures in this case were not sufficient. No one knows precisely how the base reacted, because within minutes after the invading fleet appeared in Omicron's skies the base was pounded into oblivion with beams and bombs. After the invaders landed and took control of the planet, they finished off the job they'd begun at long distance. There was not a fragment of evidence left to give posterity a clue about the actions of those valiant men and women. In addition to the loss of personnel, twenty-six ships of various sizes were destroyed on the ground, without even a chance to fight back against the unknown enemy.

As luck would have it, there were eight naval ships in orbit around Omicron, undergoing training maneuvers. They must have witnessed the destruction because, under the command of their senior officer, Captain Osho, they rallied together in a brave attempt to strike back at the invading force.

They were terribly outnumbered; the enemy strength was well over a hundred ships. But numbers meant little when weighed against the courage and loyalty of the Imperial Navy. The eight ships and their crews put up a valiant fight to protect the planet from tragedy.

Unable to make a frontal assault, the eight naval ships had to settle for harassment tactics. As the enemy fleet surrounded Omicron and pounded it with bombs and radiation, the remaining defenders swooped in from behind and made pesky little raids at their rear. It's impossible to tell whether their actions saved any lives on the ground, but they did divert some of the enemy's attention to protecting its flanks instead of putting all its energy into offense against the helpless planet below.

Once the initial bombardment had finished, the attacking fleet began to descend into the atmosphere, seeking to consolidate its gains. Again the Navy ships made daring maneuvers, almost suicidal in their willingness to weave in and out among the enemy vessels, firing shots broadside whenever a target presented itself. The invaders suffered two ships destroyed and four others disabled before they decided to put a stop to this harassment once and for all.

A detachment broke loose from the invading formation to chase down the annoying imperial craft. The Navy ships, even knowing they were outgunned, did not flee the battle. Instead, they made their pursuers chase them through the descending ranks of enemy craft. Two enemy ships crashed spectacularly as one of them chased an imperial ship a little too closely. The fiery explosion brought cheers to the defenders' lips.

But their joy was shortlived. As brave and determined as they were, they were still grossly outnumbered. They could not match the enemy ships in speed or firepower. One by one, the gallant defenders of Omicron were blown out of the sky until only two ships remained.

At this point, knowing there was nothing further they could do here, Captain Osho made the decision to retreat. The ships had been trying, ever since the appearance of the invaders, to contact some other naval bases via subetheric communicator, but the enemy was jamming the subcom channels. Presumably no other communications had gone out from the surface of the planet, either. The Empire had to be warned that this attack was taking place so it could mount a counteroffensive of its own.

The two remaining naval vessels broke off their contact with the enemy and, heading in two separate directions, made a dash for freedom. They were hoping that at least one of them could escape to spread the alarm.

Such were the overwhelming numbers of the invading force, however, that it was able to dispatch eight of its own ships to deal with each of the escaping vessels. They tracked relentlessly after their quarries, encircling them before they could get far enough from Omicron's gravitational field to slip into subspace safely.

The enemy ships englobed the two naval vessels, pouring beams of incalculable energy at the trapped craft. In both cases, the result was tragically the same: The Navy ships' shields held out against the bombardment for a few moments before finally overloading and popping out. Without that protection, the naval vessels easily succumbed, flaring in brilliant, silent explosions that scattered debris through the cold darkness of space. There was no one to take the official message back to the Empire that Omicron had been lost to a mysterious invading force.

With the last organized resistance finally defeated, the invaders must have thought they'd have a free hand – but they reckoned without knowing the spirit of the Omicronians. People living on the frontier of civilization develop a tough, stubborn nature – and the citizens of Omicron, confused and frightened as they were, were not about to surrender their world without a struggle. The Navy and its big guns were gone, but the Omicronians still clung to their little pockets of resistance.

The big cities were a shambles, but the smaller towns and villages were almost untouched by the firestorm the attackers had unleashed. Police departments around the world dragged out their heaviest weaponry and riot-control equipment in an attempt to shore up a last line of resistance. Radio communication seemed a little more reliable than subcom, and the forces scattered over the face of the planet managed to patch together some preliminary coordination of their efforts.

The invading forces seemed reluctant to land, at first. Out of the holds of the bigger battleships came scores of small fliers to flit through Omicron's skies, looking for opposition. These fliers were not heavily armed, but they didn't have to be – they faced only small, illprepared and hastily assembled militia.

Occasionally one of the pockets of defenders would manage to down an attacking flier, but that only doubled the enemy's will to wipe out resistance. More often, a few quick return shots from the flier would destroy any weapons the ground unit had, killing a few of the citizens and sending the rest fleeing for cover.

13

Within twelve hours of its start, the battle for Omicron was over. The major cities were largely piles of rubble; the few survivors in any condition to move walked about in a daze from the harsh bombardment. With the cities had gone the major spaceports and any merchant or civilian vessels that had been moored there. The smaller towns, except where a group of resisters had been blasted out, were mostly intact. The citizenry was panicked; some people fled into open countryside, while others cowered fearfully in their homes, not knowing where to go or what to do. There was no organized resistance force on Omicron worthy of the title.

Assured, finally, that they would meet no formal opposition, the invading force finally landed. The fleet of ships – of a design no one on the planet had ever seen before – touched down on a flat plain in the Long River valley. Curious locals overcame their fear to get a look at the mysterious invaders who had conquered their planet and defied the Empire of Earth.

The hatch doors on the giant ships slid slowly open – and at that moment, life on the planet Omicron was radically changed.

# CHAPTER 2
## *Proposals*

Earth was tranquil in the viewscreen, a gibbous blue globe
filling almost the entire field of view. The atmosphere
seemed like the thinnest of haloes ringing that precious
sphere, and little bits of black space, sprinkled with stars,
showed in the corners of the screen. Down below, the
Pacific Ocean gleamed in afternoon sunlight, enhanced by
a few white cloud systems. Along the zone of twilight was
the western portion of the North American continent; in
the darkness, just barely visible on the horizon, were the
bright lights of some of the bigger cities in the rockies and
the midwest.

The image was only a two-dimensional one, but that
was quite enough for the two people flying casually above
the atmosphere in the Mark Forty Service Special. They
were not interested in studying the globe in detail; it
merely served as a pleasant visual distraction to complement their more personal activities.

The cabin of the craft was small and intimate: Two
acceleration couches with but a few centimeter gap between them, surrounded by a dashboard control panel
that more resembled a spaceship's than a groundcar's.
The Mark Forty could serve as both, adding to its
sophisticated complexity. When it was in flight mode its
windows were sealed tight and became, instead, the
viewscreen that currently showed the image of Earth as
the craft orbited serenely above it.

Helena von Wilmenhorst knew it was against Service
regulations to 'borrow' a Mark Forty for purely personal
reasons. As a ranking officer in the Service of the Empire,

15

though, she was in a position to bend a few rules. She had just spent a hard sixty-hour week working for SOTE's benefit, and she felt entitled to some minor liberties.

On her left, Captain Paul Fortier of Naval Intelligence was uncharacteristically nervous. He was normally an articulate man, but tonight the handsome dark-haired officer was strangely silent; when he did speak, he frequently cleared his throat and made hesitant false starts. His conversation seemed rambling and pointless at times. He refused to look directly into Helena's face, and when she put her arms around his well-muscled shoulders she could tell he was tense, braced as though for combat.

This was not at all like the man she'd grown to know and love. They'd been working together for the past seventeen months, establishing a firm liaison between SOTE and Naval Intelligence. The two organizations had never meshed so smoothly, due in no little part to the extraordinary efforts of these two people. In fact, Helena and Fortier were discovering they meshed well personally as well as professionally.

That was why, after a long, grueling day of administrative work together, Helena had suggested they get away alone – just the two of them soaring peacefully above the atmosphere. Fortier had agreed enthusiastically enough, but as soon as they were alone in the Mark Forty he'd changed from his normally suave, confident self into the bashful, gawky man now beside her.

Helena tried gamely to carry the conversation, but after several disasters she was becoming more and more exasperated with her companion. Finally, able to contain herself no longer, she asked, 'Is something the matter, Paul?'

She could see his muscles tense still further. 'No. Uh, what makes you think that?'

'I've never seen you so wound up and jumpy. Even

16

when we knew we were going into danger on Dr Loxner's asteroid you were calmer than this.'

'Must be more tired than I thought,' Fortier muttered. 'It *has* been a long week.'

'It's been just as long for me, and I've worked as hard as you have,' Helena pointed out. 'That doesn't stop me from uttering two complete coherent sentences in a row.'

'Sorry.' Fortier looked away. 'I guess I'm just distracted tonight.'

'Maybe you just didn't want my company tonight.' Helena leaned forward toward the controls. 'We can go back down if you prefer.'

Fortier reacted quickly. He reached out and grabbed her left hand, holding it tightly and not letting it complete its intended action. 'No. I want very much to be with you. It's just . . . I'm very nervous, that's all. I've never done this before.'

'Never done what? You've flown with me before, dozens of times. All those trips between Earth and Luna Base together . . .'

'I've never proposed marriage before.' Fortier's voice was scratchy as the words tumbled from his mouth.

Helena stopped, dumbstruck for a full thirty seconds. When she finally could speak again, all she could say was 'Paul?' in a voice that did not sound at all like her own.

After spending the early evening in awkward silence, Fortier suddenly could not stop the words from gushing forth. 'There were a couple of times when I thought I might, but I never quite reached that point. There was Natasha, just as I got out of the Academy, but she suddenly got starstruck on a shuttle pilot from Patagonia and left before I even had a chance to make the offer. Then there was Kalinda, just after I made lieutenant commander – but I was offered the undercover assignment just then, and I knew it wouldn't be fair to her to have me off for a couple of years, possibly killed while investigating those pirates. She'd have had all the disadvantages of a service wife and none of the advantages. I left her without even saying goodbye, without telling her why I went. I must have hurt her terribly, but there was nothing I could . . .'

'Paul.' Helena swiveled her seat more to face him and cupped her right hand over his mouth, silencing his outburst. 'Do you mean to say you're proposing to me now?'

Fortier took a deep breath, and Helena took her hand away from his mouth again. 'That's what I thought I was doing,' the captain said.

Helena laughed and reached across to ruffle his hair. 'Idiot! You haven't asked me a thing yet.' Her movement in freefall caused her to spin slightly in the cabin, and she quickly had to stop ruffling his hair and grab at the dashboard to steady herself again.

Looking flustered, Fortier said, 'Oh. In that case, Duchess Helena Kirsten von Wilmenhorst, would you do me the great honor of becoming my wife?'

Helena's laughter stopped. Prying her left hand out of Fortier's rigid grip, she lifted both hands to cup his handsome face and looked straight into his brown eyes. 'After all the time we've spent together, after all we've come to mean to each other, did you honestly expect me to say anything but yes?'

Fortier gulped and averted his eyes. 'Well, but you're a duchess and heir to all of Sector Four. You may even end up running SOTE when your father retires. I'm just a commoner and an ordinary officer. I have no fortune, nothing in particular I can offer you . . .'

'Hold it right there, *tovarishch*,' Helena said, a spark of mock anger in her eyes. 'First of all, the Stanley Doctrine gives commoners as much right to marry duchesses as anyone else, in case you've forgotten your grade school history. Second, I don't need a fortune; I've already got one. Third, there is nothing ordinary about you. You are one of the most charming, intelligent, handsome, dedicated, talented, and wonderful men I know. You are a prize catch, and tonight I think I'm the luckiest lady in the Galaxy. The answer to your question, Captain, is a resounding yes, yes, yes!'

She pulled his face closer to her own and the two spent a long time in a passionate kiss, Helena's waist-length black hair slowly drifting in the air currents as her new fiancé's hands slid around her back. For the rest of their several Earth orbits there was nothing nervous or awkward about Paul Fortier's behavior at all.

Even hours later, when the Mark Forty had been brought back to its hangar near the Hall of State for Sector Four in Miami and the two lovers had reluctantly gone their separate ways for the night, Helena still felt as though she were in orbit. She'd been in love before, several times, but it had never worked out the way she'd always expected. In the case of Jules d'Alembert, the problem of coming from worlds with seriously different gravities had made the prospect of marriage impossible. In another case, the man had not been as serious about her as she'd been about him. Another man turned out to be merely a golddigger – a fact she'd learned just in time to prevent her making a costly mistake. Lately, the couple of times she'd gotten deeply involved she found herself having to make career decisions – and in both cases, the men came out second best to her position with SOTE. She'd almost begun to despair of ever finding the right person for her, and had poured most of her energies into her work for the last few years.

In Paul Fortier, though, she felt she'd found the perfect

match. He was a few years older than she was, mature, athletic, and very intelligent. His career also matched well with hers; they were both only too aware of the exigencies of intelligence work. Both were fiercely dedicated to the welfare of the Empire, giving them another point of shared concern.

It was true, as he himself had pointed out, that they came from different social backgrounds. Helena was from the upper levels of the aristocracy; she'd spent all her life in the glitter and glamour of the top classes, and had been raised almost as a sister to Edna Stanley, the current Empress. Fortier was from a family with a naval tradition – sturdy middleclass stock without titles or pretensions. There was bound to be some conflict in their chosen lifestyles – but given the similarity of their interests and careers, that could probably be reduced to a minimum. She was sure an intelligent person could adjust to a step upwards in society much more easily than a step down-wards.

She smiled warmly. It would be fun teaching her Paul the intricate ins and outs of protocol, the complex patterns of formal etiquette in aristocratic society. She imagined the first few dinner parties they would attend, and hoped he'd be up to making inane conversations with empty-headed countesses and half-drunk earls. She thought of the splendid reception she'd have to throw to announce their engagement – and that thought reminded her she'd have to tell her father.

She checked her ringwatch and discovered it was three in the morning, Miami time. Even with the long hours her father kept as Head of the Service of the Empire, he would probably be asleep by now. There would be plenty of time to tell him the wonderful news in the morning. She didn't think he'd raise any objections; after all, it was he who'd encouraged her to get more closely acquainted with

Paul Fortier in the first place by assigning her to work with him as liaison between SOTE and NI.

She could not later remember her drive home from Headquarters to her apartment. Her head was so in the clouds from this surprising development that her surroundings were just a blur. She'd had enough presence of mind to hook her car's controls into the traffic computer network, rather than trying to drive on her own; in her present euphoric state, she didn't want to risk an accident. She merely sat back in her seat and spent the time in pleasant reverie.

As befit a lady of her rank, Helena lived in a penthouse suite at one of Miami's most exclusive hotels. She had four, large, well-appointed rooms, maid service at her call any hour of the day, closets filled with the latest fashions, a large and timely library of bookreels, and the latest in automated conveniences. Her kitchen could handle banquets for twenty; the other three rooms had their own characteristic periods, yet each contained touches of the others so that twentieth century 'modern', Aesthetic Movement Japonica, and Deco each were clearly followed and still tastefully blended – the perfect setting for gracious entertaining.

It was everything a lady of leisure could wish. The trouble was, as she lamented to her father repeatedly, she was anything *but* a lady of leisure. Between the grueling demands of the Service and the obligatory social demands of the Imperial Court, she was almost never able to enjoy her suite. All she usually ever did here was sleep – and she frequently skipped that; her busy workload often demanded she grab mere catnaps on the couch in her office.

Helena left her groundcar nestled in its underground parking slot, still walking lightly on air from the delight of this evening. The day's fatigue was washed away. She resolved to get out of her work clothes; as attractive as the champagne tuxedo-pleated jumpsuit was, it *had* been a long exciting day. Helena looked forward to a hot whirlpool bath and a chance to lie down on her eyelet-covered flotation-bed. She wasn't sure she'd be able to sleep at all, but she owed herself the opportunity to try. At least lying down might stop the giddy spinning of her head.

She took her private elevator tube to the penthouse and pressed her hand to the keyplate. The computer scanned her handprint and recognized it as acceptable, so the door opened and she stepped from the brightly lit hallway into her darkened reception room.

Because of the headiness of that evening, perhaps she could be forgiven the few instants of bewilderment before knowing definitely that something was wrong. She stood frozen in the doorway for a moment, her instincts giving her a message that her mind was still not prepared to accept. There was a strange feeling of disorientation, as though she'd suddenly entered a world where everything was forty-five degrees from perpendicular.

Then realization came to her. The light had not come on when she entered the room. The computer had been programmed to turn lights on immediately upon her passing through the doorway. Yet if the computer were simply malfunctioning it wouldn't have opened the door for her at all. Someone must have tampered with it.

Even though Helena was not really a field agent, she'd trained at the Service Academy and the instructions they'd given her served her in good stead. She sized up the situation instantly. She was standing in the doorway to a darkened room with a bright light behind her. That made her a silhouette, an easy target for anyone inside the room. If she tried to back quickly out of the room, she would remain a target for several seconds before she could be out of the line of sight. Her best bet would be to go forward, into the darkness.

Helena dove to her right where she knew there would be a smooth patch of carpet. Once she left the doorway, the door slid silently shut behind her, enveloping the room in almost total blackness. She landed on her right shoulder and rolled until her back was against the wall. She scrambled to a crouching position, subconsciously comparing her own clumsy efforts to the smooth, fluid motion the d'Alemberts would use for the same maneuver. Her right hand reached to her belt for the ministunner she always carried there.

From the darkness at the center of the room, where Helena knew the large couch was, a woman's voice said, 'A rather melodramatic entrance, don't you think?'

'Who are you!' It took every gram of control for Helena to keep her voice steady.

'Must we play twenty questions? You know who I am.'

Indeed she did. Helena had heard that voice from only one previous source, a videotape recovered from the planet Sanctuary, but she had replayed that tape many times. The brittle coldness, the crystalline enunciation, could belong to only one person – Lady A, leader of the mightiest conspiracy ever to threaten the Empire of Earth.

With that realization came the knowledge that the ministunner she held would do her no good. Aimée Amorat had long ago transferred her mind into this perfect robot body. A stun weapon would be useless against it because she had no biological nervous system to be affected. Still, Helena kept her stunner at the ready in case Lady A had any friends with her.

Trying to remain calm, Helena said, '*Khorosho*, Aimée, I know who you are. What do you want?'

'To begin with, some common civility. If you won't yet recognize me as Empress, a simple "Your Grace" would suffice. I *was* Duchess of Durward, child, and, as such, your peer.'

23

'I'm not your child,' Helena said, 'and you're not my peer. And you still haven't answered my question.'

'You can put away your toy; it doesn't frighten me. If I wanted you dead, you'd *be* dead. I could have killed you on Sanctuary, had it suited my purposes. Killing you would serve no point; you're far too replaceable.'

Helena fumed inwardly at the insult, but remained outwardly level. Moving closer to the couch, she said, 'Then why are you here?'

'I've come to make an offer.'

'The only thing I'd accept from you is your unconditional surrender.'

'Your naïveté is beginning to wear thin, as is your presumption. The offer is for your father, not you. I trust you enough to relay it to him without getting it garbled in transmission. You should consider that a compliment.'

'I don't want compliments from you.'

'Don't wórry, you won't get too many. Sit down, make yourself at home.'

Helena's eyes were gradually becoming adjusted to the darkened room, enough to make out the dim outline of Lady A's shape at one end of the brass and leather couch. There didn't seem to be anyone else in the room. Helena thought about the blaster she had stashed in her bedroom, and wondered what the chances were of reaching it before her enemy could stop her.

'In case you're wondering about doing anything stupid,' Lady A continued casually, 'I've already disposed of the weapon you so carelessly left lying around. Now, it makes no difference to me whether you stand or sit. Your personal comfort is your own business.'

Helena twitched slightly, wondering how the woman could have read her mind, then realized that she must have glanced briefly in the direction of the bedroom. With her robot body, Lady A was much better equipped to see in the dark than Helena was; to her, the room was probably as bright as day.

'*Khorosho*,' Helena said, sitting at the other end of the couch as far from Lady A as she could. 'What's the offer?'

'Quite simply, I'm offering my help in saving the Empire.'

Helena blinked, startled. 'Are you going to betray your organization?'

'Nothing of the sort. What I'm offering is a truce and an alliance against a third party.'

Surprise upon surprise. 'Who?'

'I won't trade details with underlings,' Lady A replied. 'On your kitchen table you'll find a list of instructions on how to contact me, should your father be interested. If I don't hear from him I'll assume he's not interested in such an alliance and make my own contingency plans accordingly. Being hidden, my own organization should survive somewhat better than yours if tragedy strikes.'

Lady A stood up and started for the door.

'Wait a minute,' Helena called after her. 'Is that all?'

'Isn't it enough? I didn't want to burden you with an overly complex task.'

'Do you have any proof of what you're saying? How can we be sure this isn't just another one of your tricks?'

The other woman paused. 'Ask your father what he's heard from Omicron lately,' she said. Then the door slid open and Lady A stepped out of the room.

Helena gave brief thought to chasing after her, knocking her down, and capturing her for further questioning – but it was *very* brief thought. She was quite familiar with the capabilities of those robot bodies built by the conspiracy. They were equipped with reflexes and strength far superior to any flesh-and-blood mortal, even a DesPlainian. Were Helena to try something so foolish, she'd probably end up bruised and battered at the very least, possibly with a few broken bones as well, and Lady A would continue along as though nothing significant had happened. Cursing her own impotence, Helena watched the door slide silently shut behind the departing woman.

Helena sat in the darkness for five minutes, trying to put her thoughts in order. So much had happened tonight, from two separate directions, and she wanted to make sure she had everything absolutely straight before speaking to her father. He'd want to know every detail of the encounter with Lady A so he could know what decision to make. Helena decided to put off for a couple of days telling him about Fortier's proposal. Her happiness would be important to him, she knew, but right now he'd need to concentrate on the astonishing offer from Lady A. The safety and security of the Empire took precedence over everything else.

# CHAPTER 3

## *Summit Conferences*

As Head of the Service of the Empire, Grand Duke Zander von Wilmenhorst had almost instant access to Empress Stanley Eleven any time of the day or night. It was a privilege he tried to use as seldom as possible; knowing how precious her time was, he wanted to be sure a problem was worthy of her attention before bothering her with it.

The current situation had reached that stage of imperial notice. Anything regarding the activities of Lady A was important in and of itself – and the possibility of some other threat to the Empire as well made it doubly so. After checking all his facts, von Wilmenhorst called the Imperial Palace.

It was late afternoon, Moscow time, when the call came in. The Empress had been in the midst of a reception honoring sponsors of several major charities when a page came and told her the Grand Duke wished to speak with her on a matter of great urgency. The Empress excused herself graciously and went immediately to the nearest room with a secure communications channel.

Edna Stanley was not a glamorous woman, but she knew how to dress for stunning effect. She wore a suit of double-faced ivory silk with trapunto trim densely stitched in real gold thread. The ten centimeter cuffs were canted back to form points almost at the elbows, the gold thread holding them stiffly against her forearms. Her jacket's shawl collar was also held up by the gold stitching, framing her head and her magnificent six-strand diamond and pearl collar. She looked so impressive that even an old

27

friend like von Wilmenhorst could not help but be impressed. They greeted each other warmly and then the Empress, seeking the heart of the matter quickly, said, 'What's the problem, Zander?'

The Head relayed the story of his daughter's encounter with Lady A in the darkened apartment. The Empress listened soberly and, when he was done, asked, '*Is* there some other threat to the Empire? What does she mean about Omicron?'

'That was the first thing I checked. Sometime in the last fifty hours, all communications with Omicron ceased. Routine traffic has stopped, there have been no outgoing calls, and incoming calls are not acknowledged. I've checked with the Navy, and they tell me they've heard nothing from the base there in a couple of days. As far as anyone can tell, it's as though Omicron suddenly ceased to exist.'

'Is the conspiracy responsible?'

'It's a possibility, of course, but I'm not sure. Lady A was talking about an outside threat to the Empire from some mysterious third party. She seems to be pointing this out as an example.'

'How did she know about Omicron before we did?'

'A very good question. We know she has an intelligence network of her own, a damned good one. Perhaps this is one occasion where her people happened to be in the right spot at just the right time to learn something we didn't. I still don't like it, though, any more than you do. I take pride in the Service's reputation. We're supposed to know about trouble before it happens, not after we're told about it by our archenemies. I intend to conduct a probe into why this information came to us so late.'

The Empress nodded. Knowing von Wilmenhorst as she did, she was confident he'd find the reason behind the delay and correct it so it would not be a problem in the future. But there were other problems to deal with in the meantime.

'What could have happened on Omicron?' she asked.

The Head sighed. 'At the moment, your guess is as good as mine. It seems a good bet that Lady A knows more than we do right now, and she doesn't like what she knows. She's a woman who doesn't scare easily . . .'

'You think she's scared now?'

'It looks that way to me,' von Wilmenhorst nodded. 'Despite her bravado with Helena, her actions strike me as being inspired by worry. We know how much she hates SOTE; we've hounded her for seventy years, ever since her nasty liaison with your grandfather. Oh, she's not quaking in unreasoning terror, I grant you – but it would take a serious threat to her own security to offer us an alliance.'

The Empress paused to reflect on the matter. 'What if this is just another one of her tricks, Zander?'

Von Wilmenhorst nodded again. 'We know she's a crafty woman. She outmaneuvered us badly at your coronation and nearly managed another double-blind when she made me look like a traitor. It's been a quiet year and a half since then, entirely too quiet. I'm sure she has some tricks prepared for us, but whether this is one of them or not I can't say just yet. As always, she's given us just the most tantalizing little snip of information and left us panting for more. I'll need further input before I know how to react.'

'What do you propose to do?' Edna Stanley asked.

'With your permission, I'd like to follow her instructions and meet with her. That's the only way, apparently, to find out what she knows about Omicron. I'll listen to what she says and try to decide how smooth she's being with us. If she convinces me of a threat, I'd like your permission to agree to her proposed alliance.'

'This could be a trap, that's what I'm afraid of. What if she just wants to lure you someplace to kill you?'

'She won't kill me,' the Head chuckled. 'I'm too valuable to her where I am.'

The Empress looked startled. 'What do you mean by that?'

'Nothing sinister, I assure you. It's just that she's had a couple of decades, now, to study my way of thinking. She knows – or thinks she knows – how I'll react in most circumstances. It's like two old chess partners; after playing against one another so long, they become familiar with all the moves. If she killed me, you'd appoint someone new to run the Service, and she'd have to take a while to learn what he's like. I think she's comfortable with me.'

'If that's so,' the Empress mused, 'perhaps I *should* replace you. It would certainly spoil some of her plans.'

Von Wilmenhorst, noting her rueful half-smile, nodded gravely. 'I'm always at Your Majesty's disposal. If you need recommendations for a possible successor, I could . . .'

'Don't bother,' Edna said with a shake of her head. 'That was half in jest. I can't think of anyone I'd trust in your job a fraction as much as I trust you, whether you're predictable or not. But I still worry about you.'

'I'm glad you do.'

Edna's face became more serious as she continued, 'I can give you the first permission you asked for, to meet with Lady A and find out what her deal is. Much as I hate doing business with her, we'll have to find out what she knows and what she's up to. But as for the second – it's not that I don't trust you, Zander, but I have to keep my finger on that one personally. It's just too important. I'll listen to your recommendation, of course, but I'll reserve final authority on whether to accept her terms or not.

Listen to her offer, pry as much information out of her as you can, and then come back to me and I'll make the decision.'

'I understand,' the Head said. 'In dealing with your worst enemy, you should have the ultimate say. I'll get back to you as soon as possible.'

Edna Stanley signed off, took one deep breath, and returned to her reception. Her polite social mask was firmly in place; not a single guest at the gathering had the faintest suspicion that matters affecting the entire fate of the Galaxy were being discussed and decided while they were chatting pleasantly in the Reception Hall.

The instructions Lady A had left were quite explicit. The Head called a given number and spoke to an answering machine, stating the time he wished the meeting to take place. The Service routinely traced the vidicom number back, and found it had been assigned to a fictitious identity. The machine was one that could be called from anywhere else and have the message repeated. Lady A could not be traced back this way – not that anyone had expected to.

At five o'clock that evening, Miami time, Zander von Wilmenhorst was waiting alone at slot 36 of the Miami Heliport, just as the instructions said. He was unarmed, and the nearest people were over a hundred meters away. There was a slight whirring as a copter set gently down on the pad in front of him. Von Wilmenhorst was disappointed, but not surprised, that the pilot was not Lady A herself, but some man in her employ. At the pilot's signal, von Wilmenhorst climbed into the passenger's side and the copter took off once more.

They headed north along the Florida coast. 'Nice day for flying, isn't it?' von Wilmenhorst said conversationally. The pilot made no response, and after a few other gambits von Wilmenhorst gave up. The man had obviously been instructed to have no intercourse with his passenger; he was paid to fly, not talk.

They continued to fly north, past the beach communities that were part of the metropolitan Miami complex. After a while, they reached an almost deserted stretch of beach, and the helicopter set down once more. Von Wilmenhorst got out and the copter took off again. The Head watched it go, wondering what would happen next.

'He'll be back when I signal for him,' said Lady A as she stepped from behind a large boulder. She wore a green silk caftan – loose, flowing, totally demure and innocent. There was nothing innocent, though, about the stunning beauty of her face and the cold, merciless depth of her eyes.

'I thought we'd want to be alone,' she continued. 'By the way, since I assume you'll check, he's not part of my conspiracy, just a legitimate pilot I hired to do a job. I wouldn't expose any of my regulars to your scrutiny.'

Von Wilmenhorst approached the woman who'd caused so much grief for the Empire. 'It's a relief to finally meet you, Gospozha Amorat,' he said politely.

'We've actually met several times before, Gospodin von Wilmenhorst,' the woman said, ignoring his official title as casually as he'd ignored hers. 'That was long before you'd ever heard of me, of course. You go to so many official functions, I thought it would be amusing to be introduced to the man whose agency was chasing me so frantically. I was careful to disguise myself, of course, so I never looked the same twice.'

If she'd hope to fluster him by her admission, she miscalculated. The Grand Duke simply nodded slightly and said, 'I stand somewhat corrected. At least I am now meeting you in what passes for your true identity these days. I believe you wanted to see me about some urgent business.'

'Let's walk along the beach a little way,' she said, starting northward. Beside her, von Wilmenhorst easily kept pace. The heat of the day was fading as the cool sea breeze began to come in.

'First,' she continued after a moment, 'we must establish some groundrules. I'm assuming you're a man of your word, and that you're unarmed: I am, too. If you have any transmitting devices on your person, they're currently being jammed by some of my equipment. If any of your people try to interrupt us during our conference, I won't be responsible for the consequences. I am also assuming you've got some recording devices on you; that is acceptable. All intelligent people keep notes of important meetings, and I won't be telling you more than you need to know to work effectively with me if you choose to do so. Are we agreed on those principles?'

'They seem fair,' von Wilmenhorst nodded. 'I'd still like to know, though, why I should work with you, effectively or otherwise.'

'Humanity has been exploring space for the past five centuries,' Lady A began, 'and has been seriously expanding into the Galaxy for the last four. During that time, our supremacy has remained unquestioned. Man has been the dominant species everywhere he went. Nowhere have we found creatures smarter than, say, monkeys were on Earth.

'Suddenly, on Omicron, I think they've found us.'

The Head continued to walk beside her, silent except for the crunch of his leather-soled boots on the sand. When it became clear she expected some comment from him, he said, 'What makes you think the events on Omicron are the result of alien contact?'

Lady A found an outcropping of rock and sat down facing out to sea. The sky was darkening as the sun set behind her, and streaks of colored clouds adorned the twilight sky. 'An invading force came in and decimated the planet,' she said. 'I know it wasn't mine, and I think I can safely assume it wasn't yours.'

With some trepidation, von Wilmenhorst eyed the rock on which she sat. There was room enough for another person to sit there, but that would force him into uncomfortably close contact. There was no place else to sit except the bare sand, and that would place him in an inferior position below her line of sight. He decided to stand. 'Do you think you have a monopoly on treason?' he asked quietly.

'Of course not. But if there were any other group in the Empire that could act on this scale, I'd know about them. Taking over an entire planet is no small task, we both know that; this force did it in a matter of hours. I happen to have a firsthand account.'

'Indeed? I'd like to hear it.'

'I'll summarize it for you. One of my operatives was working on Omicron when the invasion occurred. He tells me that an enormous fleet appeared out of nowhere, wiped out the naval base and bombed the cities into submission. They seemed to have some device that jammed all subcom transmissions, so no word could be sent out. After wiping out the token opposition that was left, the ships – which, by the way, were built in a style no one's ever seen – landed and began taking control.'

'If the subcoms weren't working, how did your operative contact you?' the Head interjected.

'He had a small, one-man ship stashed away in the countryside. He was away from it when the invasion occurred, which was a lucky thing; if he'd tried to escape while all the alien ships were in the sky, he'd probably have been shot down. As it was, most of them were on the ground when he took off; he eluded the few that chased him and escaped into subspace. As soon as he was free of them, he called me and reported what had happened.'

'And he says he definitely saw these alien invaders?'

'Not personally, no. There was still a lot of chaos all around him, and people were fleeing the cities and towns in large numbers. Some of the people who passed him said they saw aliens coming out of the ships. He left before he had a chance to see any for himself.'

'What did these aliens look like?' the Head persisted with his gentle questioning.

'The reports were garbled; panicked people don't make the most reliable witnesses. In general, they seemed to be shorter than we are, humanoid in shape, with green skins, looking very strange. That was the most comprehensive description my man could get.'

'I see,' the Head replied slowly. 'And you believe this single sketchy report?'

'I'd be a fool to base my plans on anything that inexact. This report indicates there's something that requires immediate investigation, nothing more. That's why I thought we might want to work together on this matter.'

'Nothing unites people like a common enemy.'

'Precisely. Whatever the nature of this invading force, it's clearly hostile and a potential threat to the Empire. You'd want to find out what happened on Omicron anyway, correct?'

'Of course.'

'So do I,' Lady A nodded. 'If I sent out a team of my own and offered to share the data with you, you might not believe them. If you sent out your own team, you might hide some crucial facts from me. So since we both have to send out an investigative party, I'm merely suggesting that a joint venture with shared resources and information would be the most efficient action.'

'To what purpose?'

'That depends on what we find. We both have to assume worst possible case. Suppose there is a race of alien creatures intent on invading the Empire by force and seizing our planets. Suppose they have an armada of their own. Is the Empire prepared to wage a long, costly war to defend itself?'

'We'd do what's necessary. Are you offering to help?'

'Of course. I have a navy of my own, as you're well aware. I won't divulge its size right now, but it could make a significant addition to the imperial fleet if it's needed.'

'Excuse me for doubting, but your trustworthiness has never been high. Why should I believe your offer?'

Lady A looked up, staring him straight in the face. 'I've never been modest about my desires. I intend to rule the Empire, and I'll do whatever I must to achieve that. But that presupposes there'll be an Empire left to rule. If there are aliens and if they attack us, they'll be attacking the territory I consider rightfully mine. If you won't trust my word, you can certainly trust my instinct for enlightened self-interest. I don't want the Empire torn apart any more than you do.'

Von Wilmenhorst considered that. 'Perhaps I'm becoming a cynic in my old age, but all this altruism still leaves a sour taste in my mouth. Suppose we do fight these aliens, and suppose we win. What price do you intend to extract from us?'

Traces of a smile, seen by the light of a gibbous moon in the deepening twilight, curled the outer edges of Lady A's lips. 'Now that you mention it, there was something I was going to ask – only if we're completely successful, of course.'

'What is it?'

'A war can't be won solely on the defensive. Sooner or later we'll have to go into the aliens' territory if we win. I want governance of any captured alien worlds, completely autonomous from the Empire. Who knows? Perhaps I'll end up with an empire of my own, and I won't need to bother yours.'

Privately, the Grand Duke did not put any such limits on the woman's ambitions; if there turned out to be two empires, she'd simply want to rule them both. He considered it diplomatic, however, not to express those thoughts aloud.

'All this,' he said, 'is contingent on our finding a worst-case situation. You mentioned a joint venture to investigate the problem on Omicron. What did you have in mind?'

'What I *don't* think we should do is just send in some gunboats. That would just provoke another fight, and all it would prove is *someone's* there. I'd like to know a little more about the nature of the enemy – who they are, where they come from, what they're doing, what their plans are. That would require some stealth.'

'You should be good at that.'

Lady A smiled again. 'Thank you. You have a few people of your own who aren't so bad. I was envisioning a small covert assault team, three people from each side. I would be in charge of my group personally, since I'm the only one I trust fully in this matter. I'll pick two of my best people to accompany me. On your side, I'd like Agents Wombat and Periwinkle and Captain Paul Fortier.'

'I must have discretion over my choice of personnel,' the Head countered.

'This is not negotiable.' Lady A stood up and walked down to the edge of the sea, where the incoming waves just lapped at the toes of her boots. 'I'm risking a great deal, *tovarishch*, by going on this mission personally. I want to make sure I'm surrounded by people I can depend on.'

'You can depend on all three of them to hate your mechanical guts,' von Wilmenhorst said quietly.

The woman shrugged. 'If I'd wanted love I'd have chosen

some other calling. I know perfectly well what they must feel about me. I also know perfectly well that they're dedicated enough not to let their personal feelings interfere with the success of their mission. Wombat, Periwinkle, and Fortier are the three best people you've got. If I'm to infiltrate enemy territory, I want them along with me.

'Besides,' she added, turning to face him once more, 'they're the three you'd pick anyway. On a mission this delicate, you'd want people whose reports you could trust. You certainly wouldn't take my word for anything: you'll need your most dependable agents along to make sure I'm not trying to trick you.'

Von Wilmenhorst hated to admit it, but the woman was right. Jules d'Alembert and Yvette Bavol would certainly have been two of his choices, and while he might have chosen the spouse of either one as his third selection, Captain Fortier was an outstanding candidate.

Aloud, he merely said, 'I'm not empowered to accept your terms, merely to listen to them and report to Her Majesty. I'm sure she'll find them of interest.'

'Of course. You realize, though, the importance of speed in this matter. If you choose to accept my help – at least as far as the investigative mission, for now – call the same answering machine number and leave word: you'll be instructed later on meeting arrangements. If I don't hear from you within four hours, I'll assume the answer is no and prepare plans of my own.'

Out over the ocean, the Grand Duke could see the lights of the returning copter as it blotted out an increasing number of stars: Lady A must have summoned it with a silent radio signal.

'Goodbye for now, Gospodin von Wilmenhorst,' the woman said. 'It's been pleasant doing business with you – you're so much more civilized than your employees. I won't insult your intelligence, though, with any nonsense about how we might have been friends if circumstances were different.'

The Head nodded. 'No, with our respective moral codes we'd be destined to be on opposite sides of any conflict.'

'Let's just hope we're on the same side in this one,' Lady A said. 'The fate of the Empire may depend on it.'

# CHAPTER 4

## *Unwilling Allies*

Life had changed significantly for the two best teams of
agents in SOTE's arsenal since their last major assignment. Jules and Yvonne d'Alembert now had a son,
Maurice, one year old and in perfect health. Pias and
Yvette Bavol had a daughter barely six months younger:
little Kari Bavol had been named in honor of Pias's
mother.

Child-rearing on a three-gee world like DesPlaines was
a particularly demanding chore, and the two women had
been very much out of touch with their work for the
Service. Their husbands had gone out on a couple of
minor assignments together, trying to pierce deeper
behind the conspiracy's armor, but had been largely
unsuccessful. They'd broken some minor links in the
chain, but the major structure remained intact.

Fortunately the last eighteen months had been an
unusually quiet time for the Empire. If the agents hadn't
known better, they might almost have thought the conspiracy had given up its plans of conquest and turned to
respectable outlets for its endeavors. They'd learned from
the past, though, that the longer a period of inactivity
went by, the worse they'd have to pay for it later. They
found themselves in the ambiguous position of wishing
something would happen and dreading what it would be.

Jules and Yvette were getting a little itchy for other
reasons as well. While they were in their prime as agents
right now, their biological clocks were working against
them. Their younger cousins, currently performing as star
acrobats in the Circus of the Galaxy, were champing at the

bit waiting to get assignments of their own, and Jules and Yvette knew they'd soon be asked to step aside for the next generation.

Not that they'd retire, of course. Retirement was almost unheard of in the d'Alembert clan, either from the Circus or from serving the Empire in an underground capacity. Members of the family had been known to carry out assignments well into their eighties, and Jules and Yvette knew there would always be jobs waiting for them.

But being SOTE's top team of agents required razor sharp reflexes. There could be no fumbles, no mistakes. Jules and Yvette had so far avoided them, and the time to leave graciously was before they made any, while they still had a perfect record. They were hoping for at least one more major assignment though, one last great task to set a standard for the next team to aim at. What they really wanted, of course, was a chance to demolish Lady A's conspiracy once and for all, so they could hand over the responsibility to their cousins with a clean slate.

All four agents were living at Felicité, the d'Alembert estate on DesPlaines, more or less marking time. There was always something to do, and the women in particular worked out in the gymnasium to get back into perfect shape after having had their babies, but they were all quite relieved when they were summoned to the communications room for a call from the Head.

Von Wilmenhorst greeted them all warmly, but there was a strange, almost regretful look in his eyes that had them puzzled. The movements of the four agents were subdued as they took chairs around the well-worn oak conference table. Mercifully, the Head did not keep them in suspense too long. 'The assignment is just for Jules and Yvette this time,' he said, 'but I'm afraid you're not going to like it.'

'We've never expected to like our assignments,' Yvette

41

said quickly, 'but we do whatever's necessary and be glad we can help.'

'I know,' the Head nodded, 'but I suspect you'll find the conditions of this one a little more odious than most. You'll have to work *with* Lady A.'

As the agents' faces clearly registered their astonishment, the Head filled them in on the background of the Omicron problem and the need to combine forces with the conspiracy to get to the bottom of the mystery as quickly as possible. 'I've spoken with the Empress,' he concluded, 'and she's agreed to the Omicron mission at least; we're still keeping our options open regarding the larger venture until we see what we learn on Omicron. I want to hear your thoughts on the matter.'

'My thoughts on the matter are not fit for delicate ears,' Yvette said hotly. 'Lady A is an amoral, lying, murderous, cheating traitor who killed her own granddaughter, not to mention hundreds – if not thousands – of other more innocent people in her quest for power.'

'But can you work with her?' the Head persisted gently.

Jules cut in before his sister could continue her tirade. 'Yes, we can work with her – *if* she's on the level. My concern is that this is just another of her tricks to get at Evie and me. What if she doses us with nitrobarb as soon as she gets us alone?'

'You'll have your suicide capsules, of course,' the Head said somberly. 'She knows that, too, which is why I'm pretty sure she's smooth with us right now. If this is some sort of hoax, she's gone to a lot of trouble for such a tiny payoff. The situation on Omicron is real enough; her description of the events is at least consistent with our own sketchy knowledge. We'd have to investigate anyway: her suggestion of a combined mission does make some sense.'

'She always makes sense,' Pias muttered. 'That's what frightens me the most.'

'Time is short,' von Wilmenhorst reminded them. 'I have to let her know soon whether we'll work together with her on this effort. Unless you think you'd have major problems carrying out your end of things, I intend to tell her yes.'

'We'll be smooth,' Yvette grumbled in agreement with her brother. 'If it's for the good of the Empire, I can put up with nearly anything. But how far does our cooperation extend? If she doublecrosses us, I don't want to be hung out there like an idiot.'

The Head nodded. 'Perfectly understandable. You know I always give you discretionary powers. At the first clear sign of betrayal, the truce is off and you're free to take any actions you deem necessary. You're being sent along as her partners, not her lackeys: she'll have to accept that and not sell you out at some inconvenient moment.'

'That's all I needed to know,' Yvette said and, after getting a nod from her brother, she added, 'We're in.'

The Head called them back a few hours later with the rendezvous instructions he'd received from Lady A. The entire party was to gather on the planet Nereid, one of the closest worlds to Omicron. Lady A would supply the ship that would take them to Omicron; the SOTE agents would be responsible for the clothing, equipment, and weapons they brought along with them. The instant the team obtained what they considered sufficient information on Omicron, they were to leave immediately and proceed at top speed to Luna Base, where the Navy's military experts would examine the evidence they'd collected and make appropriate decisions from there.

The scheduled rendezvous was slightly more than three days from now; with Nereid being so far from DesPlaines, that barely gave them any time at all to prepare.

Since they didn't know what possible challenges they'd be facing, they had to make their selection as general as possible. For clothing they chose kneehigh dark leather crepe-soled boots and a variety of dark colored jumpsuits; they were comfortable and fit close to the body so they were less likely to snag on anything in crucial moments, and they made little if any noise even during active movement. With the jumpsuits, they each carried a utility belt with a variety of compartments filled with handy tools, explosives, some small grenades, and a few all-purpose sensors.

For weapons, they ruled out stun-guns; if they really were dealing with alien beings, the creatures might have a different sort of nervous system that would make them impervious to stunners. That left blasters as the main powered weapons of choice: There was very little that would stand up to a Mark Twenty-Nine Service blaster. For added insurance, the agents carried a throwing knife strapped to the inside of each wrist and each boot top and, in a special pocket, seventy-five centimeters of piano wire. Thus accoutered they felt reasonably prepared to deal with any menace they might face. There were a lot more devices they could have taken, but anything else would simply have weighed them down. They preferred quickness to a slight additional firepower.

The parting from their respective spouses and children was painful, especially when they knew how dangerous this assignment might be; if the alien enemy didn't do them in, their 'allies' might. All four had hoped that, whatever the next job would be, they could all work on it together – but Lady A's insistence on picking the team ruined that hope.

'I'd feel a lot better about this if you didn't have to depend on that coldblooded murderess as part of your team,' Vonnie d'Alembert said. 'She'd just as soon let you die as lift a finger to help you when you get in trouble.'

'It works two ways,' Jules said philosophically. 'She has to depend on us, too, knowing how we feel about her.'

'But she knows you're honorable,' Pias pointed out, 'whereas you know she isn't. That makes all the difference.'

The couples kissed a long, passionate farewell. Jules and Yvette said goodbye to little Maurice and Kari, wondering whether the combination of enemy forces and Lady A would allow them to see their children again. Then Pias and Vonnie took the youngsters and retired to the edge of Felicité's private landing field to watch their mates depart.

Jules and Yvette took off in their own private ship, *La Comète Cuivré*. It was a cozy two-seater, but more than that it was the fastest ship available on such short notice. In going from DesPlaines to Nereid, they would be traversing two-thirds the diameter of the Empire: even at the *Comet*'s top speed, they'd barely make it in time.

They spent a nervous three days in subspace as their ship sped along to their destination. After reading over the background files on Omicron they'd borrowed from Felicité's extensive library, there was nothing for them to do. Nothing in the history of the Empire had prepared them for the problem of dealing with a new and potentially hostile intelligent race. They moped around the ship, missing their spouses and their children, and wondering what they would say to Lady A when they finally met her face to face on an equal basis. Jules had already encountered her once – but the brief meeting on Gastonia had hardly been conducive to good relationships.

They landed on Nereid with but a couple of hours to spare. The *Comet* had a berth in it for their private groundcar and, packing their belongings into a couple of small dufflebags, they drove out of the spaceport. The local traffic computer broadcast a streetmap of the area on their car's screen, and Jules drove just a hair inside all traffic laws getting them on time to the hotel that was to be their rendezvous point.

Inside the lobby they met up with Captain Paul Fortier, the third representative of the Empire in their party. The naval officer had barely arrived on Nereid himself, and admitted to being a little groggy with subspace fatigue. Fortier had worked briefly with Yvette before and recognized her face although he didn't know her true name: even at his level he wasn't cleared for such crucial information as that. Yvette merely identified herself as Agent Periwinkle and introduced her brother as Agent Wombat. Fortier, realizing the need for secrecy, accepted the introductions and made no effort to pry further.

The three agents went into the hotel bar and sat at a table together. At precisely three o'clock local time, Lady A walked into the bar. She looked around, spotted the trio, and walked resolutely over to their table.

No matter how much they hated her, the agents of the Empire had to admit their enemy was a ravishingly beautiful woman, with black hair that was a perfect complement to the creaminess of her skin. The jumpsuit she wore was a dark forest green challis set with swirls of dark gray, and emphasized every curve of her supple form. Aimée Amorat had commissioned this robot body as the perfect receptacle for her devious mind, and her judgment could not be faulted. It was just a pity, they thought, that her sense of morals had not kept pace with her sense of style and taste.

'Since we all know each other,' she said coldly, 'I see no point in introductions. My companions are already awaiting us in my ship. Time is of the essence in this case; I'd suggest we leave at once.'

The trio followed Lady A to her groundcar and climbed in. Lady A set the computer for their destination and leaned back in her seat. The three agents sat a bit more uncomfortably.

After an awkward silence, Yvette spoke up boldly. 'I suppose you know this was not our choice of assignments.'

'Of course,' Lady A said evenly. 'It was mine. I believe in picking the best people for the job, no matter how distasteful or disagreeable they are.'

She smiled wickedly and added, 'I have no immediate intention of stabbing you in your sleep, but I suppose you'll want to sleep in shifts anyway.'

'The precaution had occurred to us,' Jules said, 'especially when we're dealing with a woman who'd cold-bloodedly kill her own granddaughter.'

The shot hit home. Lady A closed her eyes and took a deep breath for a sigh, even though her robot body didn't really need to breathe. 'It was her own wilful disobedience and stupidity that killed her. I drilled it into her head over and over that if she obeyed my commands without question or hesitation, she would end up well off. I asked for absolute faith and she did not give it. Instead, she doubted me and took matters into her own hands. She paid the price for that. The booby-trapped escape ship was meant for you. If she'd trusted me, she'd be alive today and you would be dead.'

'You say that so coldly,' Yvette said. 'Don't you feel anything?'

'How can I? I've got a machine body and a computer mind on which my mental pattern has been impressed. I have no hormones or other chemicals drifting through my bloodstream interfering with the purity of my thoughts. I had emotions once. I remember what they are. As an actress, I can even fake them most convincingly. On an intellectual level I know what I would have felt if I were still in a mortal body. Tanya was my granddaughter, my last remaining descendant. I will have no more biological progeny, no one else to pass on my spark of life. As an old woman I would have wept great tears at that tragedy.

'But in my present form, all that's superfluous. I don't need to dilute myself genetically until a paler form like Tanya emerges. My mind can go on forever. If this body wears out, I can have more built. It gives me a patience and a perspective you mortals can never match; that's why I'm bound to win our little struggle.'

'Dr Loxner thought he was immortal, too,' Fortier pointed out.

'Loxner was a foolish genius,' Lady A said. 'He tied his mind up in a cumbersome form that could neither escape nor defend itself adequately. I tried to talk him out of it, but he kept telling me what greater scope his super computer asteroid gave him. He didn't leave himself any back door. That's the key to any success, of course – a back door, a way out if things fall apart around you.'

'In other words,' Yvette said sarcastically, 'you abandon your colleagues when the going gets rough and save your own skin. That's nice to know as we head into a working relationship with you where our lives may depend on you – and yours will depend on us.'

If Lady A was perturbed by the criticism, she refused to show it. 'In this case, the success of the mission is more important than any of us,' she said. 'If the choice is to save you or get back to Earth with vital information, I'd sacrifice you without a moment's hesitation. I assume you've been trained well enough to hold the same values.'

'Certainly,' Yvette replied. 'In fact, I'd *welcome* the chance to sacrifice you.'

'As long as you keep in mind that the Empire may need me as an ally to rally my fleet if this *is* an alien attack. Ah, we've reached my ship.'

Lady A's ship stood alone on a private landing field well outside the city limits of Cochinburg, Nereid's capital. It stood impressively on its tail, nose pointed at the sky, a much bigger ship than a mere six people should need for basic transportation. When Fortier mentioned that, the woman's reply was, 'We don't know what we're heading into. A smaller ship might be faster and more maneuverable, but we need some solid defense capability as well. From the report I got, the enemy is very aggressive about patrolling the space around Omicron; my operative took off in secret, and even so barely managed to escape alive. They don't want to let anyone in to get a look at them, which isn't surprising – they want to keep the element of surprise as much as possible.

'As long as there's a chance of fighting, I want to be able to fight back. This ship, the *H-16*, is as well armed as a naval vessel three times its size. Stealth is fine, subtlety is fine, but superior firepower never hurts.'

The groundcar pulled up to the edge of the landing field, as far as the computer grid would take it. The occupants climbed out and walked across the deserted field in the long twilight of Nereid's evening. There was a slight chill in the air and the faint, unidentifiable aroma of some local flowers. Lady A set the pace leading the group toward the ship at a rate just slightly more rapid than even humans from a three-gee world could tolerate, making them half-run to keep up with her. Jules suspected that, with her tireless robot body, she was doing it on purpose to show the rest of them up.

They climbed the steep ramp into the ship itself, and the hatch closed impersonally behind them. Jules, Yvette, and Fortier exchanged concerned glances. From this point on, they would have to consider themselves in enemy territory, even when they were alone with their 'allies.' This was not going to be a comfortable mission.

Lady A led them onto the ship's bridge, a hemispherical chamber with ten acceleration couches facing consoles around the perimeter. There they met the other two members of their team. One was a man who seemed tall, although he was of fairly normal height; because Jules and Yvette were from a three-gee world and Fortier's family had also come from DesPlaines at one time, they were all somewhat shorter than average. This new comrade, though, was a well-muscled, intelligent looking chap with dark, short cut hair and thick lips that tended to scowl. He had bushy eyebrows and a nose that had been broken several times in fights. He moved with the self-assured grace of a person who could handle himself in an emergency – just the sort of ally to have in a situation like this.

The other member, though, was a surprise – a young woman shorter than Yvette and so slender she looked almost sickly. The appearance of ill-health was accentuated by the fact that she was an albino with a mane of yellow-white hair and teary, pinkish eyes. She looked as though a sudden breeze might blow her over, and she did not seem at all confident surrounded by these imposing physical specimens.

Lady A introduced her colleagues as Ivanov and Tatiana. 'Those aren't their real names, of course,' she added, 'but true identities seem to be a luxury in our circles. Only Captain Fortier and myself are being honest about who we are.'

'Meaning no offense to Tatiana,' Jules said, 'I'd like to know what qualifications she has for being along on this mission. You and Ivanov are obvious, and the three of us, but . . .'

'Brawn is not everything,' Lady A said in superior tones. 'Tatiana has a remarkable gift for linguistics. If we do end up finding a totally alien race, her talents will prove invaluable. In addition to her natural abilities, which are considerable, she's been given a computer implant auxiliary memory. Every alien symbol she sees written down, every syllable of alien speech she hears – complete with inflection – will be permanently recorded. If they use written symbols at all or speak within a sound range humans can hear, Tatiana will decipher it, given a little time.'

'I can see how her skills are important,' Fortier nodded, 'but she looks so fragile. We may be in for a rough time and hard fighting. Can she hold up under those conditions?'

'It will be our job – all of us – to see that she does,' Lady A declared. 'It won't do us a bit of good to penetrate enemy headquarters and discover we don't know the difference between their battle plans and their duty rosters. In many respects, Tatiana is the most important person on this mission. We must see to it that she's protected at all costs.'

The young woman, obviously very shy, was intimidated by so much talk about her. Her face flushed a peculiar deep shade of pink as she tried unsuccessfully to hide herself from view. Failing to escape notice, she simply said, 'I'll handle myself smoothly, you'll see. I'm not a baby. I don't have to be pampered.'

'There are obviously those of us who have more faith in you than others,' Lady A said, seeing the expression of doubt still on Jules's face. 'However, since it's a matter not subject to debate, we'll all have to live with it. Now that we're all together, I'd suggest we leave at once. Every second we lose is . . .'

'Just a minute,' Jules said. 'There's one point still to be settled.'

'What's that?' Lady A asked impatiently.

'The six of us are going into a dangerous situation. Not

only our individual safety, but the safety of the group and the success of the mission will depend on how well we work together. In moments of life-or-death crisis we can't stop to take a vote or discuss plans among ourselves. There has to be one person in the team with the ultimate authority to make snap decisions that *everyone* must obey instantly. Without that, we're bound to fall apart. We have to decide *now*, while we can discuss it calmly and rationally, just who the team leader is going to be.'

'It's obviously me,' Lady A said imperiously. 'I assembled the team. I have seniority, I have a mind uncluttered by emotions . . .'

'Kittledung!' Jules exclaimed. 'None of those things is worth a damn in field situations. What counts is experience. I'll grant you've had a lot of good experience at running and hiding – but you've never had to work on a secret mission where you had to obtain hidden information and get out alive. It's a whole different set of problems requiring a whole different set of skills and decisions to be made. I don't care how uncluttered your mind is, or how strong and fast your robot body is. You don't have the experience that counts. Fortier, Periwinkle and I do. I don't know about Ivanov, and therefore I'm inclined to doubt. But I know it can't be you.'

Lady A glared into Jules's face. Jules glared right back. For a long instant the scene on the bridge was frozen in time as two strong wills clashed in silent battle. Then, unexpectedly, Lady A smiled.

'*Khorosho*,' she said. 'I chose you for your expertise, I might as well take advantage of it. I think we can all agree on you as team leader. In *emergencies*, yours will be the one voice for the group – but in more casual circumstances, I at least will expect to have a significant say.'

Jules looked at Yvette and Fortier, who both nodded acceptance of him as leader. 'Smooth,' he said to Lady A.

'However,' the woman continued, 'this is my ship and I will pilot it. Captain Fortier may be co-pilot if you like. I gather you're something of a hotshot flier yourself, but my reflexes really do work to best advantage in this circumstance. As pilot, I expect captain's prerogative to be absolute master of my vessel. Your jurisdiction begins once we're safely on Omicron. Agreed?'

'Agreed,' Jules said. He was still in mild shock over how easy his battle with Lady A had been; he'd expected a much harder fight to win the team leadership away from her. Lady A would not enjoy taking orders from anyone, particularly from him, but she was an intelligent woman. As she'd said, she'd chosen him because he was good at this sort of thing, and he bet she could swallow her pride enough to listen to him when it mattered.

With the technicalities finally settled, they were ready for takeoff. Lady A assigned the Empire's agents to three acceleration couches within the hemispherical bridge, while she worked the ship's major controls herself. The *H-16* lifted majestically off the small private landing field, leaping into space. Despite all reservations and misgivings, the mission to learn the secret of the Omicron invasion had begun.

# CHAPTER 5

## *Stranded*

Nereid was close enough to the Omicron system that the flight would only take a few hours. They were hours the team tried to use wisely.

As team leader, Jules needed to know what resources and talents he could draw on in an emergency. From questioning Ivanov, he found the man had a varied background – professional athlete, bouncer in a number of bars, burglar, assassin and, most recently, a factotum for Lady A's criminal conspiracy. The man was hardly a model of virtue, but Lady A had picked well; he'd have the requisite skills to perform on a delicate mission like this. They could depend on him to hold up his end.

Aimée Amorat, of course, could be considered an asset to the team as long as she could be trusted. Physically, her body would be far more durable than anyone else's; mentally, she had a quick and cunning mind. She'd been an actress in her youth, and had no doubt drawn on those abilities many times in the past half century to keep herself alive and free. She had eluded the greatest man-hunt SOTE had ever staged at a time when she was merely flesh and blood like everyone else. As long as her interests were the same as those of the team, her contributions would be outstanding – but Jules would have to keep on his toes for the slightest signs of betrayal. She'd made a fool of him on Gastonia, and he was not going to let that happen again.

He and his sister, of course, worked together like the muscles in his hand. Having performed as acrobats in the Circus of the Galaxy, they were quite used to having their lives depend on each other's movements and reactions. Although Jules had never met Fortier before this mission, the officer had been a superb undercover agent in Naval Intelligence's war against the pirate menace, and Jules knew he could stake his life on Fortier's training and dedication.

That left Tatiana as the big question mark. Despite acknowledging that her talents would be needed, Jules was not happy to have her along. He learned from questioning her that she was an academician, having never been in a fight more serious – or more recently – than a schoolyard brawl. Although she seemed intelligent and widely read, she was totally unfamiliar with weaponry or the martial arts. She had an amateur's courage that might loosely be called 'pluck' – but even that could be a liability. Courage at the wrong time could be as disastrous as cowardice; only experience could give someone the discretion an under-cover agent needed so desperately.

Jules asked his sister to take Tatiana aside and give her at least a rudimentary education. Yvette gave the young woman some basic advice on how to fall without hurting herself, how to hold a knife in a fight, and how to handle a blaster. In the closed confines of the ship, though, there was noplace they could use for target practice; there'd be no way to tell until they were actually in the middle of trouble just how good Tatiana's aim would be.

In the meantime, Jules conferred with Lady A and Fortier on possible strategies. The trouble was, too much was still unknown to formulate any definite plans. Lady A's reports had said that the major cities were all but wiped out, but there was no indication of where, if anyplace, the invaders had established a base of their own. There was no way of knowing how well the enemy had fortified their position in the days immediately following the takeover, and how alert they'd be at spotting the incoming ship. The best approach would be to come in fast and as low as possible, just skimming the atmosphere and keeping an eye out for two things: possible attack from sentry ships, and groupings of enemy structures on the ground that might indicate a main base of some sort. They would have to improvise from there on – but Jules was used to that.

All too quickly came the warning from the ship's computer that they had reached the Omicron solar system and it was time for the ship to leave subspace. The crew of the *H-16* strapped themselves into their acceleration couches and Jules, Yvette, and Ivanov took up gunnery controls on the ship's weaponry. Once they were back in normal space almost anything could happen, and they had to be prepared for it.

The ship slipped out of subspace in one of the smoothest transitions Jules had ever experienced. Much against his will he had to admit Lady A was a superb pilot; she had done the astrogation for them all the way from Nereid and brought them out barely a million kilometers from Omicron itself – an achievement of accuracy that made a hole-in-one at golf seem trivial by comparison.

The *H-16* sped through space toward Omicron at top speed. Paul Fortier kept a sharp eye on the sensor screens, alert for the slightest sign that their entry into Omicron's space had been detected. Lady A, too, was watching those screens, ready to react the instant any enemy blips appeared.

They flew on silently for several minutes, and the tension on the bridge became almost tangible. It would be too much to hope for that they could approach and land unscathed. It would make their job easier, of course, if the enemy didn't suspect there were infiltrators on the planet, but at this stage of the game the assault team could count on nothing.

Gauges measuring the ship's hull began showing a climb in temperature, indicating they'd reached the outer fringes of Omicron's atmosphere. The *H-16* was not really designed for rapid atmospheric maneuvering, so Lady A made fine adjustments to put their vessel into a tight polar orbit around the planet. They were high enough that they had a wide field of view beneath them, and yet low enough that their screens could search for and detect any large agglomeration of buildings that would represent either a human town or a possible enemy base. By comparing the landscape below with the maps of Omicron already in the ship's computer, they could find any new settlements that might be alien in origin. It was unlikely the aliens would have built any large bases in the week since they'd taken over, but if even a large part of their fleet had landed in one given area it would be noticeable to the orbiting observers.

Tatiana was given the sensitive task of checking the monitors and comparing everything to the original maps. At this altitude, and with the wide angle field of view, it would take about twenty hours to fly over all the land areas at least once. They considered it most unlikely they'd be given twenty hours before the enemy spotted them and gave chase, but there was also a chance they might get lucky and spot the enemy base more quickly. At least this aerial reconnaissance was worth a try.

The landscape below, as shown on the screen, left a depressing effect on all of them. Several times they passed over large cities, and even from this altitude it was clear they'd been reduced to rubble. Imagining the thousands, if not millions, of people who must have died in that attack, it was all too obvious that this enemy threat must be stopped, or else this devastation would be repeated on planet after planet throughout the Empire as the enemy made its advance. Jules and Yvette could see now why

Lady A was as eager to stop this menace as the Empire was – her own interest was very much at stake.

'Unknowns approaching.' Fortier's level voice broke the heavy silence of the bridge. He read off their course coordinates from his computer screen, then added, 'They're bearing in fast; we'd best assume they're hostile.'

Even before he'd finished speaking, Lady A had set the ship into accelerated motion once again. Her hands fairly flew over the control panel in front of her, so fast they were little more than a blur. Although Jules had most of his attention focused on his artillery controls, he was able to watch her out of the corner of his eye, and had to admit he was impressed. Even with his DesPlainian reflexes he would not have been able to react so quickly to the situation at hand. Much as he hated to admit it, she'd been indeed the perfect choice to pilot this vessel.

The *H-16* blasted out of its stable orbit and began an elaborate series of evasive maneuvers, and the crew inside felt the pull of acceleration from different directions and different magnitudes. They were all strapped tightly into their couches, so the changes did not send them flying about the cabin; even so, the continual jolting made it difficult for them all to concentrate on their respective tasks, particularly the three team members working the gun controls.

Without taking her eyes from her own console, Lady A gave the order, 'Fire at will.' At the gunnery controls, Jules, Yvette, and Ivanov all acknowledged the command. That had been assumed all along. Their only chance of landing safely would be to shoot the instant anything came within their scopes. An enemy who bombed defenseless cities neither gave nor deserved quarter.

The enemy fighters came on fast and hard. Unlike the *H-16*, these were built for speed and maneuverability, and they came zipping in with one goal in mind – the destruction of the offending vessel. By comparison, the *H-16* was a behemoth – slow to turn, slow to change course, but also possessed of heavier weaponry. As the enemy fighters closed in, the *H-16* got its chance to show what it could do.

Gunnery in space was a particularly exacting skill mastered by very few. Imagine: You have a target capable of moving swiftly through three dimensions, and of accelerating or decelerating from moment to moment. This target is likely to take evasive action to avoid being shot by you. At the same time, your own craft is undergoing other directional and accelerational changes of its own. The same effect could roughly be achieved by letting the air out of a balloon and then trying to shoot at it from the back of a bucking horse. The results were generally more frustrating than gratifying.

It was hardly surprising that the majority of shots in any space battle missed their marks completely. On those occasions when an enemy target lined up precisely in the sights, the gunner's own ship was just as likely to make some maneuver of its own just as the shot was fired, ruining the aim. Being an accurate space gunner required not only superhuman skill and superhuman reflexes, but superhuman patience as well. A fluent knowledge of off-color language was considered optional, but handy.

Jules, Yvette, and Ivanov sat with their attention riveted on their individual screens, waiting for the precise instant a target offered itself. There might be only a fraction of a second that one of the enemy ships slid within range; they would have to spot it, direct the computer aiming module, and fire all within that split instant. They could not be concerned with piloting their own craft; they had to put complete faith in Lady A to handle that chore successfully. The sharp motions of the

*H-16* were unavoidable distractions, but their concentration was strictly on the field of view covered by their detectors.

As the enemy craft came within range, the *H-16* let off a few shots just to let the attackers know they meant business. Undeterred, the enemy fighters kept coming. Jules had one of the ships directly in his sights and fired quickly, but Lady A chose that second to veer from her course and Jules's shot went wide. That same maneuver, however, brought the other ship into Yvette's screen, and her shot was perfect. A beam of intense energy burned its way from the *H-16* through empty space until it hit the enemy ship's hull. The defensive screens were no match for the power of the *H-16*'s blast; they blew out on contact, and the beam pierced the hull. The two vessels were moving at such great relative speed that even the fraction of a second that the beam existed was enough to rip a long gash in the side of the other craft. There was the strange silent explosion that was an eerie hallmark of space battles, and this one enemy ship was no longer a threat to anyone.

Yvette did not see the damage her shot caused; the ship was out of her viewer again by the time it exploded and she was watching for any sign of the other vessel. It was not until Fortier cried, 'Hit!' from his own viewscreen that she felt the satisfaction of knowing she'd done her job well.

That feeling was replaced by dismay just a moment later, however, as Fortier called out, 'Three more coming in.'

In short order the fighting became fast and furious. The enemy craft were laying down a fire pattern of their own, and it took all the speed of Lady A's computer reflexes to steer a course safely through the barrage. Deciding the low orbit region above Omicron was temporarily dangerous territory she pulled out and headed on a course that would loop around Omicron's single large moon and back again. The attacking craft naturally followed. Yvette and Ivanov knocked out two more of them along the way, and no new ones were immediately dispatched. That left the large *H-16* against two smaller fighters as they disappeared from the planet's view behind the moon – just about an even fight.

As soon as they'd been eclipsed by the moon, so the enemy base on Omicron couldn't know what was going on, the *H-16* swung around. No longer was it merely a vessel running for its life, it was actively on the attack for the first time. It bore straight in at one of the attackers, giving all three gunners in turn a clear shot at the enemy's flank. Three consecutive beams lashed out from the *H-16*'s blaster turrets and one of them – no one was ever quite sure which – hit its mark. Out of control, the damaged enemy vessel plunged down onto the surface of the airless moon, creating a spectacular new crater on the already pockmarked surface.

Keeping to a straight course for that long a time, though, meant the *H-16* was a more predictable target, and it paid a penalty for that. The remaining ship sent out a beam that caught them a glancing blow along the nose. The *H-16*'s shields were stronger than would ordinarily be expected in a ship this size, but even they could not withstand the strong input of high energy coming from the enemy vessel. The shields blazed gloriously for a moment, then flared out completely. The ship shook with the impact of an explosion, fortunately minor, as the beam destroyed the *H-16*'s attitude maneuvering jets.

In just that instant the Empire team lost half their ability to dodge successfully, making them that much more vulnerable to attack. Lady A knew several tricks to compensate for the loss, but given the speed on the other fighter it might not be enough. The enemy seemed to have detected this damage, because the craft came twisting in at a steep dive in an all-out bombing run at its disabled foe.

Disabled it may have been, but the *H-16* was still far from helpless. As the fighter homed in along its path, its course took it in and out of Jules's screen at irregular intervals. He could take the chance on firing discrete shots, as was standard in warfare; with his quick reflexes, there was a reasonable chance he'd hit the vessel. But if he didn't there was a better than even chance it would destroy the *H-16*.

Instead he chose to be unconventional. Disconnecting the timer cutoff, he fired a continuous beam into a point in space along the other ship's path, and held it for a full fifteen seconds.

The drain on the ship's energy was considerable. To channel that much power into one blaster beam meant diverting it from elsewhere. The ship's damage assessment computer, realizing that the attitude controls were nearly gone, took all the power from that system, but it wasn't nearly enough. Lights went out, sensor screens blanked, even the main drive faltered as energy was diverted into the single ray issuing from Jules's turret. At the control panel, Lady A swore as the ship responded but sluggishly to her commands. Jules's own screen was flickering badly, and for a while it was difficult to tell whether his gamble had any effect.

Then the beam hit the enemy ship, and there was no doubt at all. The bright explosion registered on all the screens with a flash that made everyone shield their eyes. Jules stopped firing and connected the timer once more. Even so, it took several seconds before the ship's computers were able to readjust the powerload and bring conditions on the bridge back to normal.

Lady A swiveled her acceleration couch, glaring at Jules. 'That was a damned reckless thing to do!' she shouted at him across the cabin.

'Yes,' Jules said, unruffled, 'but it worked.'

'The agreement was that *I* controlled the ship while we're in flight.'

'Exactly. You said fire at will, and I did.'

Unwilling to spend further time in pointless argument, Lady A turned to Fortier. 'Any further opposition?'

'None on the screens,' the officer answered. 'Who knows what'll be waiting for us when we get around to the front side of this moon again. If we stay on this course unaltered, that'll be in about seven minutes.'

While listening to him, Lady A had continued to test her instrument panel and asked for a quick computer assessment of the damage to their ship. '*Khorosho*, time for a quick decision. Our maneuverability is severely impaired, which will hinder us in any fight. We could leave and get another ship, but that delay is unacceptable to me. The alternative is to make it down in this one. That's what I choose to do.

'The enemy may have more ships waiting just on the other side of the moon, in case we emerge victorious. They may be waiting to hear from the ships they've already sent out before dispatching more. We can count on nothing but our own speed to get us through.'

She called up on her screen a quick scan of the Omicron maps again, watching the scenery flash past until she found a spot she liked. She entered its location into the computer and almost instantly the ship returned the course she would need to reach that point.

'Since we don't know precisely where their base is, if indeed there is one, we'll have to land somewhere and find out more details on the ground. I've chosen a spot near a conflux of smaller towns and not too far from Barswell

City. The city was probably decimated but the villages may be intact. At the least, there may be other transportation to take us where we need to go.'

'What about *this* ship?' Yvette asked.

'If it gets us to Omicron, it will have served its primary function. I intend to crash it.'

There was a silence in the cabin as she made that announcement. It was up to Fortier to state what was on everyone else's mind. 'That'll leave us stranded on Omicron. How will we get back to the Empire to make our report?'

'There will undoubtedly be means available,' Lady A said calmly. 'If we're at all successful at finding the critical information, it means we'll have penetrated the enemy base. They'll have ships there we can use.'

'Assuming, of course, we know how to work their controls,' Jules said, adding his objections to Fortier's.

'That's why we have Tatiana with us, to decipher these things,' the woman replied. 'Or there may be small private ships on hand somewhere that haven't been destroyed. If we can't escape physically, perhaps we can find a way to send out a subcom message past the enemy interference. There are alternatives open to us. The alternative we no longer have is to play more games of hide-and-seek with this ship.

'Even more to the point,' she went on, 'the enemy currently knows we're here. Until they know we've been dealt with one way or another, they will continue to search for us. A ship that crashes with sufficient violence to leave no wreckage and no bodies may satisfy their curiosity about us, at least temporarily. In these circumstances, we'll need every advantage we can get.'

'Sounds like you intend to stage a pretty showy crash,' Yvette said. 'How are *we* going to walk away from it?'

'By not being in the ship at the time, of course,' Lady A said scornfully, turning back to her controls.

For the next several minutes there was too much action to allow conversation. The *H-16* accelerated along its course and sped out from behind the cover of Omicron's moon once more. Much to their relief, the team found no reception committee waiting for them, just a vast ocean of empty space between themselves and the planet. As they zoomed back toward Omicron, though, Fortier announced several more small ships coming up to intercept them.

Without the attitude units there was little the *H-16* could do to dodge the oncoming vessels. Instead, Lady A set her controls for maximum acceleration and charged right into the teeth of the enemy attack. The shields were gone, and a direct hit would mean the end of the mission, but they had no other choice – moving slower would only make them an easier target.

The ship's lack of evasive action made the gunners' work that much easier. Jules and Yvette each scored a hit on one of the enemy's fighters, and the rest of the attack force backed off a little more cautiously to see what the result of this suicidal charge might be. They had obviously not been in contact with their comrades on the other side of the moon, so they could not know the *H-16*'s attitude controls were out. They thought this was merely another tactical maneuver, and they waited to see what would come of it.

The *H-16* hit the upper reaches of Omicron's atmosphere and kept on going in at top speed. It would have been the rankest suicide to charge directly down through the air; the ship would have burned up in a flash like a bright meteor. Instead, their course was a steep downward spiral: Their rate of descent was carefully calculated to keep the friction temperature on the hull within the metal's tolerable limits. They zoomed past the enemy ships who were still expecting them to make some tricky move. Realizing they'd been outmaneuvered, the remaining ships took off in pursuit behind the descending *H-16*.

Lady A set the preprogrammed course into the ship's autopilot and turned to face the rest of her crew. 'The time has come for us to depart,' she said. 'Follow me.'

Ivanov and Tatiana obediently unstrapped themselves from their acceleration couches and walked after their boss. Still somewhat mystified, Jules, Yvette, and Fortier followed suit. They knew Lady A was not the suicidal sort, and she had told them she always believed in having some escape route planned. They would have to trust her sense of self-preservation to save them as well.

The *H-16* made occasional random acceleration changes to avoid being hit by enemy fire, and this made walking through the ship's corridors difficult. Just when a step seemed secure, the ship would lurch and throw everyone off balance. The crew had to make sure they had a firm grip on some handhold before making the next tentative step forward, or risk being tossed about the hallways.

Following Lady A's lead, they climbed awkwardly toward the rear of the ship to a special compartment she opened up for them. 'Here we have our escape module,' she said almost cheerily. 'We'll leave the ship in this.'

'Won't the enemy just see us separating and send some of the fighters after the module?' Fortier asked.

'The landing spot I picked has heavy cloud cover, so they probably won't spot us visually. As far as most standard sensors go, this craft is invisible. It's made almost entirely of nonmetallic materials – glass, ceramics, wood, and various plastics – so most of the detectors humans use wouldn't notice it. There's only tiny traces of metal in a receiver screen, not enough to register. Of course, if these are aliens and use radically different instruments we could

66

be in trouble, but I doubt it; everything we've seen so far is at least comparable to our own technology.'

'How did you make a nonmetallic engine?' Yvette wondered.

'I didn't,' Lady A replied with mounting impatience. 'This module doesn't have an engine – that's one less way it could be detected.' She held up one hand to forestall the next obvious question. 'And no, we won't drop like a rock. In atmosphere, this module acts like a glider. Now stop questioning and get inside.'

The escape module had not been built to hold this many people comfortably. There was one pilot seat, which Lady A took for herself, and a benchlike rim in a semicircle behind it for the other five people to crowd onto as best they could. Ivanov, the last person in, sealed the module behind them and gave his boss the signal that everything was ready.

On an instrument board below the cockpit window, Lady A watched the monitor screen to check their progress. As she'd told them, the *H-16* was rapidly approaching a dense cloud bank on its furious descent to the surface of Omicron. She waited patiently until the proper moment and then, the instant they hit the clouds, she pulled back on a lever in front of her.

The lever released a catch that held the glider in place within the ship's hold. Instantly a hatch sprang open in front of them and a series of springs propelled the module at great speed out the hole and away from the falling ship. For better or worse, they were now irrevocably committed to the planet Omicron.

The change in their environment was startling. One moment they were in the hold of a ship, the next they were gliding free in the air. The gray-white of the clouds came whipping by them, and there was a sudden drop in both temperature and air pressure. Even with so many bodies pressed closely together, the chill of a stormcloud in the upper atmosphere permeated the glider's insulation and soaked through to their bones.

The egg-shaped module shared the *H-16*'s downward speed at the time of separation, and for several seconds they plummeted through the clouds toward the hard ground below. Then, just as they broke through the cloud cover, Lady A pulled back on a second lever and a set of wings unfolded from the body of the egg beneath them. Their little craft shook and shivered as it caught the violent air currents below the clouds.

They were in the middle of a driving rainstorm. Even though they were on the daytime side of the planet, the thick layer of clouds above them obscured the sun and made the sky gray and leaden. Now that they were below the clouds they were pelted by hard droplets of rain and a bit of hail that had not dissolved at this altitude. The rain streaked the windshield and obscured visibility so badly that Lady A had to ask Tatiana to work the wipers manually from a lever inside the cockpit.

The day was so dark they could barely see the ground, spread out below them like a shadowy diorama. They were over farm country that looked completely untouched by the enemy invasion. Large rectangular fields covered the terrain like a patchwork quilt in differing shades of yellow, green, and brown. The land was mostly flat, with a few gently rolling hills off in the distance. The tranquility of the scene, even through the driving rain, seemed to belie the dire circumstances in which Omicron now found itself.

The enemy fighters continued down after the *H-16*; none of them peeled off to follow the glider, so Lady A's ruse seemed to have worked. On the dashboard receiver, cameras from the ship transmitted images of its final moments.

A beam from one of the enemy vessels lashed out and touched the *H-16*'s hull. It would not ordinarily have been a fatal blow but Lady A, wanting to leave no evidence of their escape from the ship, had rigged the *H-16* to self-destruct the instant it was hit by enemy fire. The scene on the glider's monitor suddenly went dark as the ship exploded in a thunderous blast of white-hot vapor.

The glider's passengers, though, had little time to contemplate such matters – they were too busy holding on for their lives. The violent air currents that comprised the rainstorm rattled the tiny craft with teeth-jarring intensity. Shearing winds threatened to rip the glider apart at any moment; the glider bucked, rolled, and pitched worse than any rollercoaster.

Even with her superhuman strength, Lady A had to fight to maintain control of the glider. The craft rolled over completely several times, and the mechanized controls seemed to have a will of their own. The five passengers behind the pilot's seat were buffeted back and forth against the walls and each other till they were thoroughly sore. Still the glider kept falling at a rate that seemed far too fast for the passengers' comfort.

Jules and Yvette exchanged worried glances. Had Lady A's vanity led her into taking a gamble even she couldn't pull off? Seated behind her as they were they couldn't watch the expressions on her face, but her body posture seemed as unyielding as ever as she struggled with the balky controls. Not for the first time the agents regretted placing their lives in her hands.

At last, when they were barely half a kilometer above ground level, the storm relaxed its grip. The rain eased slightly from a downpour to a monotonous beat against the glider's body and the winds, while still harsh, were manageable by a skilled pilot – which Lady A certainly was.

Ivanov pointed to starboard. 'Town at two o'clock,' he called.

They could all see a small cluster of buildings just on the horizon indicating one of the villages they knew should be in this area. Lady A saw it and nodded, then veered the craft slightly to port. Her reasoning was clear; they didn't want to bring the glider down too close to the town because they might be seen and the enemy could be alerted once again to their presence. As distasteful as it was, they would have to land somewhere in open country-side and walk into the village.

They circled the area for a while, riding the unpredictable winds, until Lady A found a site that pleased her. She wanted something smooth and open to provide an easy landing field, yet close enough to shelter that they could cover up their glider and camouflage it from aerial inspection. They didn't want some enemy pilot spotting the vehicle by accident; the longer they remained undetected, the better their chances of succeeding in their mission.

At last they found what they wanted: A broad open field in which to land, bordered by an orchard in which the small glider could safely be hidden from aerial view. There was always a chance it would be discovered by someone on the ground, but they didn't have the tools to bury it. At least their craft would not be in casual sight.

They spiraled in for a landing, watching the land flow beneath them like a kaleidoscope. As they came lower the buffeting by the rain and the crosswinds increased once more, but Lady A handled the controls with an expert touch and kept them on an even course. Jules found himself looking at her with regret that she was such a cold, vicious person – she had so many skills and talents that could be put to use in better ways than scheming to overthrow the Empire.

On their final approach, Lady A released the landing

gear and the wheels came down and locked into place. The whole group braced themselves as they came flashing through the field at a speed that seemed far too great, while Lady A lowered the flaps to give them as much braking power as she could.

The little craft bumped and jounced its way through the rows of crops and over the uneven ground. A wheel on the port side hit a pothole and threatened to spill them over, but Lady A quickly countered by turning the wheel into the new direction, veering their course and heading them straight for the trees. The glider finally rolled to a stop twenty meters from the edge of the orchard, and everyone breathed a great sigh of relief.

Lady A pulled back on the lever to fold the wings into the escape module's body once more, at the same time releasing the catch that held the canopy in place. The top of the egg sprang back, and the people inside got their first whiffs of the clean, cold air of the Omicron rainstorm.

Despite the downpour they were all eager to get out of the cramped confines of the tiny cabin. Within a very few seconds they were all soaked to the skin, wet hair plastered to their heads; even the normally majestic Lady A could not overcome the ravages of the weather – she looked as much like a drowned rat as the rest of them.

Before doing anything else, they had the task of pushing their glider into the orchard. The module was surprisingly light, but the uneven ground made pushing it a laborious chore, even for all six of them. Lady A was the only one not puffing by the time they finally had the craft hidden some distance within the orchard – but then, being in a robot body, she didn't need to breathe at all.

For the first time since encountering the enemy fighters, they had a chance to review their situation critically. With the loss of the *H-16* they were stranded indefinitely on Omicron, a planet dominated, if not controlled, by enemy

71

forces. They had only the clothes on their bodies and the equipment they'd brought with them to use in fighting the unknown menace. They were cold and wet and didn't know exactly where they were. As the beginning for an important mission, this was not exactly the most propitious.

# CHAPTER 6

## *Capture*

At Jules's command, the team set out in the direction of the town they'd seen from the air. They stayed inside the orchard as long as possible to take advantage of the trees' cover, but after only half a kilometer the orchard ended. They would have to walk the rest of the way to the town under open sky in full view of any invaders who might fly over. Jules thought briefly of waiting until dark, but decided against it. Speed was more important here, and the sooner they reached the town and started finding out what had happened, the better their mission would go. If anyone spotted them from the air, there was no way to tell they weren't ordinary citizens of Omicron.

The chill and the rain made them feel miserable. They had dressed for stealth, not for warmth or comfort, and they were regretting that decision. Their hair was stringy and wet, dripping down their noses and cheeks; their breath formed small clouds of steam in front of them. Each step became an effort, as they had to lift their feet out of the mud and step right back into it again. Fortunately they were all wearing boots to keep their feet reasonably well insulated, but the constant slogging in addition to the generally dreary climate only depressed their spirits more.

Tatiana, with her delicate metabolism, was affected worse than the rest of them. Her body was wracked by a continual series of shivers, and even though she tried her best to keep quiet Jules could hear her teeth chattering a couple of meters away. His chivalrous instincts came to the fore, even though Tatiana was associated with Lady

A's conspiracy; he wished he had some sort of cape or other garment to cover her and protect her from the worst of the rain. But he was dressed no better than she was, and could do nothing to help her.

The only one not affected by the weather was Lady A. Her normally elegant hair was as stringy as everyone else's and her clothes were just as soggy, but that hardly mattered. Jules presumed she had some sensors in her skin to inform her of its condition, but in a robot body she could ignore external discomfort. She walked through the muddy fields with her normal proud posture, head erect and back straight. She slowed her pace to match her companions, but it was clear she could have outdistanced all of them had she chosen to.

After about an hour's walking the rain finally stopped and the late afternoon sun broke through the clouds for a few moments. They found a wooden fence to rest on, and Jules called a temporary halt to their march. They regained their breath and rested their legs while Lady A stood by, aloof and barely tolerant of her comrades' physical infirmities.

'I'd like to reach the town before nightfall,' she said after a few minutes' silence. 'I can see perfectly well in the dark, but the rest of you would be handicapped if we ran into any trouble. Besides, we might find a place to dry off. I prefer not to look like a soggy sponge.'

'How are you feeling, Tatiana?' Jules asked. The young woman was their weakest link and it was she, not Lady A, who would have to set the pace. As Lady A herself had said, Tatiana was the most important member of their group and Jules was going to make sure she wasn't pushed beyond her limits.

'I can go on,' Tatiana said, making a show of bravery.

'Don't let her bully you,' Jules added. 'We can take as long as you need.'

'I'll be smooth, really,' the woman insisted.

Jules was still not sure, but he was reluctant to press the matter any further. As they started forward again, he caught the wisps of a smile on Lady A's face, but he refused to let it bother him.

Another fifteen minutes' walk brought them to a road, which enabled them to increase their speed dramatically and was a great relief to all of them. Shortly after that they spotted some buildings up ahead to indicate the outskirts of the town.

No vehicles passed them as they walked along the road, and as they neared the first group of buildings they sensed a quiet that bespoke abandonment. There was no movement, no activity to indicate this was a place where people still lived. At a cautionary word from Jules they slowed their pace and approached the town warily.

The first couple of buildings were stores dealing with farm supplies – a grain and feed store and a shop that specialized in tools and farm machinery. Both had been locked up tight and abandoned. Across the street, a combination repair shop and garage was also shut, but it had been broken into and looted of tools. A few meters further down the road, a small grocery store had been completely ransacked; people fleeing the town had wanted to take plenty of provisions with them.

As they walked up the road into the heart of the town, the story remained unchanged. Everywhere around them, buildings had been closed up in a hurry; depending on their contents, some had later been broken into by people needing the supplies they contained. Further into town, the road became a more formal street, complete with sidewalks and houses lining the sides, but there was still no sign of the inhabitants. Cars, too, were nonexistent; all available vehicles seemed to have been grabbed in the general exodus.

75

Small animals scampered through the streets ahead of them. Not knowing much about the local fauna, it was hard to say whether the creatures were pets who'd been deserted or some of the larger vermin that had become bolder in the absence of people. Most of the animals were skittish and stayed well away from the humans, which was fine with Jules; he hadn't come here to conduct a wildlife survey.

The sun was just setting when they came to a store that sold fabric and clothing. The door was ajar; the building had been partially ransacked, but most of its inventory was intact. The team entered and found toweling to dry themselves off. The jumpsuits Jules and Yvette had brought along were sturdy, and when dry would be as good as new. Lady A's bodysuit seemed similarly durable. The other three team members, however, looked very much the worse for wear, and they took this opportunity to change into newer and better outfits. Yvette made sure Tatiana selected good clothing that would keep her warm and dry.

Jules felt guilty about simply taking merchandise from the store, so he left a note explaining that SOTE would pay for the articles they'd taken. Lady A watched him without comment, but there were traces of a bemused smile on her face.

A few doors away they came to a restaurant. It had been many hours since they'd eaten, and everyone except Lady A was ravenously hungry. The restaurant had been vandalized, too, but not all its supplies had been taken. Yvette volunteered to be chef and, even though most of the foods were strange to her, she managed to cook a pretty decent meal that filled them up.

It was completely dark by the time they finished eating, but the street lights had come on outside, indicating that at least some of the town's automatic mechanisms still functioned. They debated staying in the restaurant for the night, but there wasn't any place in the cafe to sleep comfortably. Instead they went down the street and broke into one of the larger homes, where they found beds that were more to their liking.

They were all dead tired, but Jules insisted they make arrangements for sleeping in shifts. He and Lady A would take watch for the first shift, Fortier and Ivanov would take the second, and Yvette and Tatiana would take the third. With that decided, the group settled in for the night.

When they were alone, Lady A turned to Jules. 'I can understand that the rest of you need to sleep, but I see no reason why I should waste my time here with you. I can probably cover the rest of the town while you're sleeping and give you a thorough report in the morning.'

'Part of the reason I'm here is to verify what you say,' Jules told her. 'I can't do that if you go off on your own.'

'I'm merely going to eliminate the inessential,' she argued back. 'By combing the city while the rest of you sleep, I'll save you valuable time. If I find anything of material interest, I'll make a note of it and we can all explore it together in the morning.'

That made a certain amount of sense – but Jules had learned to be cautious whenever anything related to Lady A made sense. 'What if something should happen to you while you're off by yourself?'

Lady A gave him a cold smile. 'You needn't worry about that, Comrade Wombat. I've always been quite good at looking out for myself.'

And without giving him a chance to argue further, Lady A slipped out the door and was gone, leaving Jules alone. He was upset, and knew he shouldn't be. What she'd said made perfect sense. They were in a hurry on this mission, and as long as she didn't need to sleep there was no reason why she shouldn't do some independent exploring – as long as she shared her findings with the Empire team afterwards. At any rate, there was nothing Jules could have done to stop her short of using his blaster. Like it or not, he'd have to learn to trust the woman who was the Empire's archenemy.

The night passed without incident. Lady A returned at sunrise with a pleasant surprise – a large groundcar capable of holding them all in some comfort. 'At least we won't have to wear ourselves out with long hikes any more,' she said.

'I'd begun to wonder whether there were any cars left in town,' Fortier said.

'I found this in a garage for repairs. I spent most of the night fixing it up for us.'

'So now you're a mechanic, too,' Yvette cracked.

Lady A looked at her unflinchingly. 'When you've lived as long as I have, you learn a lot of things.'

'Well, *I'm* glad we won't have to walk,' Tatiana spoke up in defense of her boss.

'Any sign of the enemy?' Jules asked quickly, hoping to break up the growing animosity.

'No, nor any traces of the natives. The town's been deserted, as far as I can tell.' Lady A was all business again. 'This is consistent with what my informant told me. He said everyone was running away from the cities, hoping to hide out in the countryside.'

'Perhaps we should try to track some of them down,' Ivanov said. 'They might give us eyewitness accounts of what happened.'

Lady A shook her head. 'We know what happened. We want to know what *will* happen. The people hiding in the country can't help us do that. We have to find the invaders and infiltrate them to learn their plans.'

They went back to the restaurant for a quick breakfast,

and then set out once again. Lady A drove the large groundcar at speeds that made even Jules and Yvette breathless. The conspiracy's leader relied on the super-swift reflexes of her robot body to maneuver the car at a rate no flesh-and-blood human would safely attempt. They were out of the small town in no time, cruising down the paved road toward the next village.

A couple of times they thought they spotted motions along the side of the road, people running and hiding at the sight of the car. Lady A ignored those distractions and drove on. Her reasoning was that the people who ran and hid were not the people they were here to see. It was the invaders who boldly took what they wanted that interested her.

Once an aircraft flew overhead, and for that they did stop. The six of them quickly piled out of the car to catch a glimpse of the vessel as it flew past. It was a vehicle of a design none of them had ever seen before, and they had little chance to see it now: It zipped by and over the horizon in just a few seconds. If it had spotted them, it obviously was not interested.

The next town they came to was a virtual replay of the first – quiet, open, abandoned by its citizens. There was no sign that any of the invaders had been here, but the townspeople had taken no chances. They'd escaped while it was still possible from an enemy that showed no mercy.

They found some maps in the town and learned that they were now only a few kilometers outside Barswell City. After a short conference, Jules and Lady A agreed it was in their interest to view some of the damage from the initial bombardment firsthand. Even if the invaders weren't there, it would give some indication of the unknown enemy's destructive capabilities. That would be most useful in devising any military strategies for combating this menace.

It was Fortier who spotted the walking tower first. He saw it as a speck on the horizon – but it moved, and that caught his peripheral vision. He pointed and the others looked, too – and Lady A immediately swung the car off the road to pursue in that direction. The land around was relatively flat, so the car had little trouble maneuvering through the fields. When they came to fences, Lady A drove through at demon speeds, relentless in her pursuit of this promising object.

It was not until they got closer that they could appreciate the tower's size. It was built roughly like an oil derrick, seven stories tall, with the metallic legs carrying it in great land-devouring strides. Atop the derrick was a round, flattened plate like a circular observation deck. Some of its surface was white, while other parts were reflective silver. It was impossible to see inside, but that didn't mean it was impossible to see out.

'Not so close,' Yvette cautioned. 'We don't want them to spot us.'

'From that height, if they haven't already seen us they're too blind for us to worry about,' Lady A replied as she drove with her customary abandon. 'It's merely a question of whether they consider us important enough to bother with.'

'There's still no point in tempting them,' Fortier said. 'I've seen enough soldiers on patrol to know that even if they don't consider us a threat, they might decide to use our car for target practice.'

Lady A ignored the comment and drove on after the tower. The point quickly became moot, however, as the car hit a patch of mud left over from the previous day's rain. The car skidded around in a full-circle turn and one wheel became mired, spinning uselessly and throwing up great globs of mud.

By the time they all got out and freed the car once

more, the tower was gone. There was hope for a future encounter, though, since it had been headed directly into Barswell City where the team was already going. They drove quickly back to the road and continued along their previous path, anticipating their first close encounter with the enigmatic enemy.

The outskirts of Barswell City looked undamaged, but they too stood deserted. As the team drove further into the metropolitan area, there were more piles of rubble to give evidence of the bombardment. The smell of death became almost overpowering: thousands of bodies left unburied for a week beneath tons of debris made a nauseating stench that left the five flesh-and-blood members of the group gagging.

'We'd better not stay here too long,' Jules choked out. 'Dead bodies harbor diseases; we don't need any additional complications at this stage.'

The further they traveled into the city, the more impassable the roads became. Lady A had to slow their vehicle practically to a crawl to avoid rubble strewn across the street, and sometimes had to backtrack and take an alternate route when the road ahead was completely blocked. None of them wanted to get out of the car and investigate the ruins on foot; the stench was too noxious, and it was already abundantly clear how thorough the invaders' bombardment had been. Any planet falling to their attack would suffer horrible casualties.

They rode mostly in silence, both out of respect for the dead and in awe of the enemy's power. One unanswered question hung heavily in their minds: Where were the invaders? Aside from the brief encounter with that walking tower and the fight with the scout ships when they approached the planet, there had been no sign of the people who had caused this devastation. What could be their reason for bombing the life out of a planet's cities and then leaving the ruins untouched? What did the enemy want so badly that they would go to these horrible lengths to achieve it?

Eventually, having decided they'd seen enough, they drove out of the central city area into the outlying region of homes again. They were discussing whether to look for a copter and fly to other cities in their search for the invaders when they heard some far-off sounds. These were the first artificial sounds they'd heard, other than their own, since crashing on Omicron, and they turned in that direction immediately. At least it promised something more than the depressing desolation they'd seen so far.

For a while, they couldn't see what was happening, because there were too many buildings still standing in this part of the town. As they came closer, though, the nature of the sounds became clear. A battle was going on somewhere in the suburbs. Highpowered energy beams were being exchanged and buildings were crumbling as they took the brunt of the fighting. Encouraged, Lady A accelerated the car and took off in that direction.

As they rounded a corner, the walking tower came into view once more. Still several blocks away, it dwarfed the houses and apartment buildings that dominated the neighborhood. Blaster beams sizzled down from the disk-shaped compartment on the top, aimed at a point out of the team's sight. There seemed to be some return fire, too, coming up from the ground, but the beams were much paler than the tower's. Jules guessed they were from handheld blasters or blaster rifles at most – scarcely the sort of firepower any defenders would need against that tower.

Lady A stopped the car a couple of blocks away from the fighting. 'No sense providing them with too choice a target,' she said. 'We'll be much more discreet if we walk in from here and see what's going on.'

They climbed hurriedly out of the car and ran toward the

scene of the battle. As they approached within one block, the situation became much clearer.

The tower had taken a position in the middle of a small park. The defenders were across the street, in what had been a row of houses. Some of the two-story structures were still standing, while others had been blasted into rubble which the defenders used for cover. The defenders kept hidden most of the time, which made it hard to estimate their numbers, but Jules would have guessed there were somewhere between twenty and forty of them. As far as he could see, they stood no chance at all against the enemy's war machine.

'The machine's concentrating all its fire over there,' Yvette pointed out quietly. 'I could slip in behind it and climb up one of the legs. If I can't break into the disk itself and take out some of the operators, I've got enough explosives in my belt to knock out one of the joints and topple it over.'

'Absolutely not,' Lady A said. 'We came here to observe, not fight in hopeless battles.'

Jules decided to use his position as team leader to put in a word on his sister's behalf. 'Maybe the people who ran to the countryside can't help us, but these people have been battling the enemy face to face. They can tell us what sorts of weaponry they have and what their tactics are. If we can link up with them, and maybe capture some of the invaders for ourselves, we'll be ahead of the game.'

'There are better ways of getting the information we need,' Lady A insisted.

Jules nodded. 'I'm sure there are. But none of them are available right now. Speed is the key to this mission, as you've said more than once. We can't wait for opportunities to present themselves – we have to make our own.'

He turned to Yvette. 'Go to it – but be careful. Bail out at the first sign of trouble.'

Yvette gave him a brief nod and slipped from their hiding place, zigzagging her way across the rubble-strewn street. She took every opportunity to stop behind some cover so her approach would not be noticed.

The park in which the tower stood had been decimated by the initial bombardment and the current fighting around it. There was no cover worthy of the name to hide Yvette from view once she crossed the street. Steeling herself, she made a dash at full DesPlainian speed across the open ground, hoping there would be no guns trained on her. The gamble paid off: She made it without incident to the base of one of the tower's seven-story legs.

From this point it was simply a matter of climbing – a snap for an old circus trouper like Yvette Bavol. The legs were bare metal structures – no attempt had been made to ornament their functional design. The naked girders and bolts made easy handholds as Yvette scampered up the leg like a monkey up a tree. Her only concern was that the tower would start walking again; anything approaching the speed it had been moving before would surely dislodge her and send her plunging several stories to the ground. Fortunately, the tower's operators seemed content with their strategic position and were not inclined to move from it.

Jules and the others watched from their hiding place as Yvette made her daring climb. Jules would have liked to be along with her, but knew that would be stretching their risks a little too far. Besides, someone had to stay back and keep a rein on Lady A.

When Yvette was three-quarters of the way up, another factor entered the picture. O ' of the sky, seemingly from nowhere, swooped one of those strange aircraft the team had seen earlier. It ignored the tower and made a strafing run at the resisters' hiding places. A combination of bombs and beams hammered at the defenders' position.

Some of them were forced to retreat, while others stubbornly held their ground against the barrage.

The plane was gone as abruptly as it had come, but it unquestionably left its mark on the battlefield. Physically the defenders had suffered serious casualties and the piles of rubble they were using for cover were smaller and more jumbled. Emotionally, they were shaken. When they could be attacked so devastatingly from an unexpected quarter in so short a time, it was hard to press on with the fight. Death seemed the only sure outcome, and retreat seemed a better alternative. Still, the Omicronian pioneer stubbornness kept them fighting on when others might have turned and fled.

Yvette made it to the top of the tower's leg, just below the passenger disk. She studied it closely for any possible opening she might have, but the machine was too well sealed against external force; there might indeed be some way to get in, but finding it would take more time than she could afford. Frustrated, she turned her attention to the tower's external structure and met with more success.

The legs were attached to the disk at the top by a complex series of socket joints, enabling them to swivel rapidly at many angles. Reaching into the compartmentalized utility belt she wore, she pulled out a series of small explosive charges. It took every bit of her fantastic acrobatic abilities to climb around the joint, setting the charges in places where she calculated they'd do the most damage. Then, scurrying around to the other side of the tower, she set off the explosives.

There was no loud roar; the explosives were not that powerful. They were, however, accurately placed for maximum result, and that was what Yvette got. The 'shoulder' of the tower trembled for a moment, then buckled and caved inward. The tower tilted precariously, more and more of its weight suddenly falling on the disabled limb. The crew inside made a frantic effort to readjust the three remaining legs into a tripod arrangement, but offbalance as they were they couldn't quite make it work. The tower twisted slowly around and began to fall.

Yvette clung to her precarious perch as the tower toppled with an exaggerated slowness. She held her spot while the tower fell, judging distance with a keen aerialist's eye. At the very last moment, while she was still about two stories above ground level, she pushed off with a mighty leap and soared through the air. She landed well clear of the falling behemoth, tucking herself into a ball and using the momentum from her fall to roll her safely along the ground.

Beside him, Jules could see Lady A nodding almost imperceptibly. 'Impressive,' she said beneath her breath. Jules smiled. There were still a few tricks he and Evie could show her.

The smile vanished an instant later as the top of the tower hit the ground. The group was unprepared for the violent explosion that rocked the street, bringing down a few more buildings with the sheer magnitude of the blast. An enormous fireball erupted into the sky, followed seconds later by an angry cloud of dense black smoke. The air for hundreds of meters around heated up to summer temperatures and stank of burning plastic.

'So much for our chances of capturing any of the invaders alive,' Fortier muttered.

Stunned by the blast, it was all Yvette could do to scramble to her feet and run for cover, in case more explosions or fires followed. In the confusion she ran toward the line of the city's defenders rather than back to her own group. It didn't seem to matter: the only direction of immediate importance was away from the fallen tower.

The defenders, who had also witnessed her act of bravery, welcomed her into their ranks.

Then, diving through the black cloud, the enemy aircraft came again. This time it delivered neither bombs nor blaster beams against the brave band of militia. Instead, like a cropduster, it left a trail of smoke in its wake, a thick yellowish cloud that settled heavily on the ground. A few of the defenders farthest along the flight path had time to see what was coming and get away, but most of the people – Yvette included – were caught up in the yellow cloud.

The Empire group across the park could hear the sounds of coughing, but the yellow smoke was so dense they couldn't see what was happening. The gas dissipated quickly, though, and they could see bodies sprawled haphazardly across the rubble. At this distance it was impossible to tell whether they were dead or merely unconscious.

Jules jumped up to run to his sister, but Lady A grabbed him tightly by the shoulder and held him in place. He started to protest, but she merely pointed to the sky in the direction from which the enemy plane had come.

A bigger, slower craft was settling to the ground near the sprawled bodies. Although it, too, was of a strange design, it reminded the team members of nothing so much as a transport copter. As the vehicle touched down, a door opened in its side and a team of creatures emerged. They were all wearing bulky suits to protect themselves from any vestiges of the yellow gas, and it was impossible to tell much about them other than the fact that they had two arms, a head, and walked upright on two legs. In height they were slightly shorter than an average DesPlainian, but they seemed much more slender.

Moving quickly, the spacesuited figures began picking up the bodies and carrying them quickly into their waiting aircraft. A couple of them picked up Yvette and began carrying her unceremoniously in with the others.

'We've got to save her!' Jules exclaimed.

'How?' Lady A asked coolly. 'It'd be suicide to charge that ship. I won't allow it.'

Looked at from the logical side of his mind, Jules had to admit she was right. To make a direct run at the craft would take him across some fifty meters of exposed terrain; it would be foolish to think they wouldn't spot him and shoot him down before he could reach them. He could circle the perimeter of the park, taking advantage of cover afforded by rubble and old houses – but at the rate the creatures were working, they would be finished loading all the bodies by then, and they might already have taken off.

'We've got to do something,' Jules muttered. 'Maybe a diversion.' His mind started thinking along convoluted paths, of having a few members of the party go off to one side and start creating enough disturbance to allow the rest to move in and perform the rescue. But there wasn't the manpower, the equipment, or the time, and Jules knew it.

'I didn't want her going on that fool's errand in the first place,' Lady A said smugly. 'We can't risk any more of our people trying to save her.'

Jules clenched his fists in anger and watched, frustrated, as the enemy figures finished their task. The last of them hopped back aboard the transport craft, and the vehicle took off once more into the afternoon sky – carrying Yvette with them.

# CHAPTER 7

## *The Omicron Liberation Army*

'At least we can be sure the gas didn't kill her,' Lady A commented as the enemy vehicle vanished from view.

'How can we know that?' Tatiana asked.

It was Jules who answered glumly, 'The invaders would hardly go to the trouble of picking up dead bodies – not when they've already left so many lying around after the bombardment.'

'But what do they want with them?' Ivanov asked.

'Interrogation, ransom, slaves, sacrifices, food, or experimentation,' Lady A said calmly. 'At least, those have traditionally been the reasons for taking prisoners throughout human history. If these are indeed alien creatures, they may have come up with some new permutation.'

Jules shot her an angry glance. 'You're so comforting.'

The woman shrugged. 'I'm not afraid of voicing the unpleasant truth. You knew it as well as I.'

'I think we ought to go looking for some of those defenders who managed to get away,' Fortier said, trying to defuse the touchy situation. 'They've spent the past week fighting the enemy; they may be able to fill us in on some of the background.'

Jules nodded slowly. He needed something to take his mind off Yvette's predicament for the moment. 'Good idea,' he said. 'Maybe they even know where the enemy base is or where they take their prisoners.'

Flames were still engulfing the disk that had been atop the enemy's walking tower. The team skirted around that and went across the park to where the defenders had mounted their courageous stand against the fearsome war machine. The yellow smoke had completely dissipated by now and the five members experienced no ill effects. They did note that, while the enemy figures had loaded the bodies of the fallen defenders into their vehicle, they had left the weapons behind. Apparently they were not too concerned about the damage any survivors could do to them.

The streets were once again as silent as those of the other villages they'd visited. The other people must be around here somewhere, but they'd retreated to some hiding place to lick their wounds after the battle.

Jules and his team could have spent days trying to find the particular hiding place the defenders were using, but there just wasn't the time to waste. Cupping his hands to his mouth, Jules cried out, 'Hallo, where are you? We're friends, we want to talk to you.'

When that brought no immediate response, the five members of the team continued on through the deserted streets, calling aloud to the people they knew must be there. After twenty minutes they were starting to grow hoarse when they finally got results. A blaster beam sizzled the ground a few meters in front of them, coming from the second-story window of a house on their right.

'Hey, don't shoot, we're friends!' Jules called up to the unseen sniper.

'Prove it,' a voice called back.

'Do we look like some of *them*?' Fortier asked.

'No,' the voice admitted. 'But maybe you decided to work for them.'

'One of our party knocked out that tower, and got captured for her efforts,' Lady A said imperiously. 'Does that sound like we've sold out?'

'Was she with you?' The voice was a little awed; Yvette's stunt had obviously made an impression. After a moment of silence, a door opened downstairs in the house the blaster fire had come from. 'Come on in, then. Anyone who'll fight like that is welcome.'

The Empire team accepted the invitation and entered the house. Inside, everything looked preposterously normal considering the planet had been brutally invaded and conquered. Modern furniture was spaced judiciously over a hardwood floor with a thick hooked area rug in the center of the room. The only jarring note to the decor was the stack of blaster rifles leaning up against one corner.

There were ten people in the room as the team entered, and more joined them within a few minutes from other parts of the house. Most of them carried blasters tucked inside their belts. There were men and women ranging in ages from early twenties on up. There were no children, but Jules hadn't expected to find any; children would probably have been evacuated to the countryside, far from the scene of any battles.

The strain of the past week was evident in the faces of Omicron's defenders. Even though Omicron was as far from the center of galactic civilization as it could get, it was far from a rough-hewn pioneer world. Life had been reasonably comfortable here until the sudden invasion. Without warning these people had been thrown into a desperate battle for survival, a battle that for many of them had been until now little more difficult than working at a daily job and deciding what to make for dinner. Despite facing a ruthless enemy and overwhelming odds, despite overcoming their ignorance of fighting and military techniques, despite being disorganized and undisciplined, these people had held together and put up a valiant struggle. Every one of them deserved a medal, Jules thought, looking around. It was amazing the heroism even 'ordinary' people could find in themselves when the need arose.

One large-boned woman with gray-blond hair, in her mid-forties, was evidently the leader of the ragtag army, even though her well-worn Marine uniform showed only the rank of staff sergeant. 'Welcome to the Barswell City Division of the Omicron Liberation Army, such as it is,' she said with a tired good humor. 'I'm Meg Maguire. Sorry about shooting at you, but we're all a bit on edge these days. It doesn't hurt to be too careful.'

'I can see that,' Jules said. 'You've done miracles just to stay alive, let alone fight back against the enemy.' He hesitated just a second before introducing himself, not wanting to mention his real name in front of Lady A. He finally decided on using one of his previous cover names she'd heard before. 'I'm Ernst Brecht, and these are my friends – Paul, Aimée, Ivanov, and Tatiana.'

'Glad to meet you,' Maguire said. 'If you can fight one-tenth as good as your friend, you'll be welcome indeed. That sure was a pretty sight out there, to watch her bring that tower down. Shame they had to drop the gas when they did,' she added with a shake of her head. 'We sure could have used more like her, but she's gone now.'

'Where did they take her?' Jules asked. 'What will happen to her?'

'Slave camp, most probably. Nothing we can do about it. Just cut the losses, shore up the barricades, and fight again tomorrow.' She spoke with the world-weary expertise of someone who'd spent her life in battle, not just the past week.

Maguire invited the team into the dining room, where she and some of her people sat around the table to exchange information. She offered them a local beverage that tasted like iced coffee with a strong aftertaste of vanilla, and while they were relaxing she filled them in on her background. Lady A had asked about the uniform, and Maguire explained she'd been a sergeant in the

Imperial Marines for nearly twenty years before an exotic ear infection on the planet Nampur affected her equilibrium and forced an early retirement. She'd come to Omicron two years ago with a good pension, looking forward to a quiet, orderly existence owning her own sporting supply shop. Until the invasion she'd done pretty well for herself. When the chaos hit, her military training came to the fore. Gradually she built up around her a group of people who would rather fight the enemy than run and hide in the country. There were few real opportunities for battle, since Maguire's people had little transportation and the invaders seldom came into the city. Today's was only the third skirmish, and the first in which anything substantial had been accomplished thanks to Yvette's bold action.

Maguire finished her story and looked expectantly across the table at Jules and Lady A, whom she recognized instinctively as the two leaders of the team. It was obvious she wanted a comparable story about their own background before she'd trust them any further.

Jules wanted to tell her the truth, that they were a team sent by the Empress herself to investigate and report on the Omicron invasion. But he knew he dared not say that. It wasn't that Maguire and her people were untrustworthy; quite the opposite, in fact. But if any of them were captured, as many were this afternoon, they might be interrogated and made to tell about the mission. It would never do to let the enemy know a team of infiltrators was busy behind the front lines, and that the team consisted at the moment of a mere five people with a sixth already in custody.

So instead he made up a story, borrowing heavily on the research he and Yvette had done about Omicron on their way to Nereid. He and his friends were from West Lenton, a city halfway around the globe from Barswell

City; they'd been on a camping trip in the Umhall Mountains when the invaders hit, and consequently they didn't know much about what was happening. When they could no longer pick up any commercial broadcasts they got worried and started heading in toward civilization again. They passed a number of people fleeing the cities and heard some strange horror stories, but they were resolved to learn the truth with their own eyes. Today had been their own first encounter with the invaders, and they were suitably impressed.

Lady A sat quietly while Jules talked, letting him make up the story for them all. She knew better than to interrupt, which might introduce some contradictions into his tale. She would trust him to play the hand correctly in this circumstance.

Jules encouraged Meg Maguire to tell them more about the enemy – what sort of machines did they have, what kind of weapons did they use, did they have any weaknesses, did they have a base anywhere and, above all, what did they look like?

The invaders were not human, Maguire assured them of that. Several people had come to Barswell City from the country and from other nearby cities, and they'd seen the creatures emerge from their ships. The reports matched pretty closely to what Lady A had already heard: These alien beings were humanoid in appearance but generally shorter, the tallest being barely a meter and a half high. They had skin that was pale yellow-green and pear-shaped heads with large, hyperthyroid eyes. Their bodies seemed smooth with no body hair – at least none that anyone had seen. They usually wore heavy clothing covering everything except their faces; a few people speculated that meant they came from a warmer climate and were cold even in the temperate regions of Omicron.

Technologically, they seemed to be on a par with the

humans. They used energy weapons similar to blasters, and while they used different forms of air and ground transportation, they worked on the same scientific principles as human craft. They had that yellow smoke that acted as an instant sleep gas, much the same as tirascaline, and they apparently had some device capable of jamming subetheric communications over the enitre planet because no messages in or out of Omicron had been delivered since the invasion began. The most chilling advantage the aliens had was a ray that seemed to sap a human's will and leave him powerless to resist. 'That's how they keep the slave camps in order,' Maguire said.

'You mentioned slave camps before,' Jules said. 'What exactly are they? Where are they located and how do they work?'

'We don't know too much,' Maguire explained, 'because no one's ever escaped to let us know what happens inside. The only person in our company who's ever seen one was Rajowiscz; he passed it on his way here from Fallstown.'

'Can we talk to him?' Fortier asked.

'Unfortunately, no. He was one of the people caught by the yellow smoke a few hours ago; he's probably in the camp himself by now. He said he spied on it from a hill for almost an entire day. The camp is a big compound made up of inflatable tents that might house a few thousand people in cramped conditions. He said he saw hundreds of people being forced to work for the aliens, constructing a series of buildings. It looked to him like they might be making themselves a base of some sort.'

'Where was this?' Jules asked.

'About seven hundred and fifty kilometers southeast of here, in the Long River valley. The strange thing was, he said, there weren't any fences around the area, yet no one tried to escape. He saw someone get out of line just once, and the aliens shone some kind of ray on him and he stopped all his resistance immediately. Whatever that thing is, it must be pretty effective.'

'Slave labor is a very inefficient work force,' Tatiana spoke up. 'If these aliens are as technologically advanced as we are, they should have plenty of automated construction equipment to do the job better.'

'But the construction equipment and materials would have to be brought here,' Lady A pointed out, 'whereas the slave labor is already here for the taking. If their invasion force is primarily fighting ships rather than transports, they'd have limited space for bringing in heavy machinery. If they have a ray that makes people their slaves, they know they can count on an unlimited supply of native workers. The cheapness and easy availability would more than offset the comparative inefficiency.'

By now it was dinnertime. The army's cooks had provided an evening meal, and the Empire team was invited to join the regulars – an invitation they certainly didn't refuse. The meal was a rough one, prepared under the most adverse of conditions. The bombing of the city had disrupted both water and power; food had to be cooked over an open wood fire, and water had to be brought in with great difficulty from reservoirs outside of town. Still, Maguire's army managed to keep itself going and have enough left over to give its hospitality to strangers.

During the dinner, Maguire made the invitation Jules had been expecting, that ꬶ two groups should team up to fight the invaders together. The romantic part of his soul longed to accept the offer; it would be a fine and noble calling to fight for freedom against these heartless tyrannical monsters. At the same time, he knew he had to put his talents to use in a much more important mission, getting information about the invaders back to the Empire so it could wage the larger battle effectively.

It was difficult saying no – not because he didn't want to, but also because, on the surface, he had no over-whelming reason. He couldn't tell Maguire about their mission, and any other excuses sounded weak even to his own ears. He finally ended up telling her that they were looking for family and friends from whom they'd been parted when the invasion began, and they had to find out whether the missing loved ones were still alive and well. Maguire looked skeptical, but accepted Jules's refusal with good grace. She added the invitation for the group to spend the night here in the house, and that was one invitation they could accept.

Tatiana asked whether the army had captured any of the aliens' equipment, and Maguire showed her a few artifacts they had on hand. Tatiana studied the markings on them for a few minutes, then handed them back with a polite thank you. They were not enough to decipher an entire alien language, but they were the first real clues to be stored in her computer-assisted memory for later decoding.

In the morning, with sorry farewells, Jules and his comrades left Maguire's headquarters and set out back toward their car. Along the way they passed the fallen tower in the park, and they paused to examine it more closely now that the fire had finally gone out. In the bright sunlight it looked less alien than it had in yesterday's afternoon shadows.

Twisted bits of metal had been thrown everywhere by the fireball explosion, and it would have taken an army of experts weeks to piece together the way the interior of the passenger disk must have looked. There was no sign whatsoever of the disk's inhabitants – if, indeed, there'd been any – but they found some twisted pieces of paneling that looked as though they might have come from control boards. Tatiana studied them with an experienced eye.

'These symbols are repeated under a number of what look like switches,' she pointed out. 'They might be the symbols for "Off" and "On." Those other symbols on dials might be numbers. They seem to use colors to indicate meanings, too; see, this panel was divided into five different color stripes, each with its own set of symbols. It's a fascinating problem.'

While she was studying the panels, Ivanov made a major discovery: Tucked into a hidden compartment in the wall of the disk was a series of cards. Each card illustrated some diagram that might have been a control, with a long set of writings beneath. The cards were charred about the edges from the heat of the explosion, but being tucked away in a sealed compartment had kept them from being totally destroyed.

Tatiana's eyes widened with delight as Ivanov brought the cards to her. 'An instructional manual!' she exclaimed as she glanced quickly through them. 'We could hardly ask for anything better.'

'If it's like some instruction manuals I've seen,' Fortier said, 'it'll only make things more complicated. It's hard enough to read them in Empirese.'

They found nothing else of value in the wreckage, and walked back to their car. Tatiana was busy studying her instruction cards with rapt attention, and was lost to the rest of the world. For the others, though, a decision was brewing. It was left to Ivanov to broach the question as they neared the car. 'Where do we go from here?'

Jules looked at Lady A. 'I think we ought to find the Long River valley and see what's happening in that slave camp.'

'Your suggestion is no doubt motivated by thoughts of rescuing your partner,' she said coolly, 'but it's nevertheless a useful one. Maguire said the slaves were being used to build some kind of base. We're more likely to find the information we need visiting that than we are by driving around these deserted cities. I trust you'll keep your priorities straight, though; rescuing Periwinkle is at best of secondary importance compared to the task of gathering intelligence on the enemy's plans.'

Jules had his own opinion of Lady A's priorities, but he kept it politely to himself.

# CHAPTER 8

## Slave Camp

Yvette awoke with a splitting headache and a feeling of total disorientation. The arteries in her neck were throbbing with pain; each pulse brought a new stab to her mind. The world seemed to be spinning around her, and it took a few minutes for her to realize she was lying still on her back on a lumpy surface that turned out to be a pile of other bodies, some of which were starting to move themselves.

She opened her eyes and turned her head, and even that simple action produced a wave of nausea she was barely able to control. She coughed a couple of times, and each cough produced new waves of pain into her head and waves of nausea out from her stomach. She couldn't recall having felt this bad since a bout of nipsum fever she'd had as a teenager. To overcome her sickness, she tried to focus her mind on the world outside herself.

The place she was in was dimly lit, and smelled heavily of many unwashed bodies. The air was warm and stuffy, and there were the sounds of other people breathing, coughing, gagging. At least one person off to the left was experiencing the same nausea she was; there was the sound of retching and the unmistakable odor that only multiplied her own queasiness.

People started moving amid groans of pain, and the floor of this darkened chamber became a writhing mass of humanity. No one quite had the strength to stand, yet, but a few like Yvette were starting to look around them and assess their situation.

Then suddenly a door was opened and the room was

filled with the blaze of late afternoon sunlight, blinding in its intensity to eyes that had grown accustomed to the previous darkness. The light only stabbed worse into a head already throbbing with pain, and Yvette blinked back her tears, trying to prepare herself for what might come next.

A couple of figures appeared in the doorway, silhouetted against the light. Even though she couldn't make out any of their features, Yvette knew instinctively that they weren't human beings. There was a slight awkwardness to the posture, a slight difference in the ratio of limb-to-body size that set them easily apart in her mind. The heads were a strange shape, and not at all attractive.

One of the beings shouted something at the waking people, a word Yvette couldn't make out. When no one responded, the being fired an energy weapon at the ceiling, flooding the room with even more light and heat. The point was not lost on the people in the room; even as groggy and sick as they were feeling after the effects of the yellow smoke, they scrambled to their feet and faced the door. At a curt gesture from their captor with the gun, they marched out of the room, into the daylight.

They'd been confined in the hold of some kind of transport vehicle, currently situated on open ground. The place around them was a center of feverish activity, people moving about on various errands. To the right and in front were long inflatable buildings, like mylar blimps growing from the ground. They weren't laid out in the usual human grid pattern, but in a strange, alien system that made no immediate sense. A river ran past a few hundred meters to the left, and beyond that, in the distance, was a range of hills. This region had once been meadowland bordered by forest, but the ground had been trampled underfoot by the constant slogging of thousands of feet, and the trees had been cut down and uprooted.

The end result was a mostly level stretch of dirt, devoid of any natural character.

The ground would not stay empty for long, though. Over to her right, beyond the inflated buildings, Yvette could see a more permanent structure rising. It was still too incomplete to show any final details of its form, but it did look strange to her sophisticated eye.

That one quick glance was all she was permitted at the moment. The alien with the gun barked another order, and all eyes in the group trained on him. He pointed in the direction of one mylar building, leaving little doubt in anyone's mind they were supposed to move that way. Yvette walked along with the rest of them; this was neither the time nor the place to challenge someone with a blaster.

As her head began clearing from the yellow smoke's aftereffects, she took stock of her personal situation. The aliens had taken away her blaster, yet had left almost everything else intact. Her utility belt was still around her waist, and most of its compartments – including the ones with the minigrenades – appeared untouched. Even the four knives she'd brought with her were still strapped securely to her wrists and inside her boots. With this equipment and her own native abilities, she could put up a fight against some pretty strong opposition.

She was surprised and more than a little puzzled. Either her captors were terribly careless or else they showed a remarkable lack of concern about how much resistance could be offered.

The captives were lined up single file in front of a table. Each in turn had to kneel while one of the aliens placed a slim metal collar around his neck. It was a simple and streamlined procedure, and the line moved quickly until it came to Yvette's turn.

The DesPlainian looked the situation over. One of the

102

aliens was seated at the table, placing the neckbands on humans. Two armed aliens stood behind the table watching the crowd and prepared for trouble. There were more of the aliens scattered around within a hundred meter radius, all armed with strange but impressive-looking weapons.

Yvette knew she could kill the three aliens at the table with a few quick movements, but where would that leave her? There were more who would instantly draw their weapons. Even if she could avoid all of them, she had no place to go. The area had been worked flat, offering little cover to a fugitive. She had no idea where on Omicron she was, or how she could rejoin her brother. She would be on foot, fleeing a ruthless enemy whose sneak attack had savagely killed millions of innocent people. A few seconds of defiance would lead to an early grave.

Beside, she had come to Omicron to find the invaders and learn what they were up to. Now that she'd achieved the first objective, it would be a waste of a good opportunity to run away. Even if she wasn't in the best position to learn everything she wanted, she was alive and in the middle of an enemy base of some sort. That gave her something to work with.

With only the slightest of hesitations, Yvette knelt before the table. The alien seated there leaned forward and placed one of the thin metal collars around her neck. The being's skin felt cool and somewhat greasy against her own, and she had to brace herself not to flinch. The collar clicked into place around her neck, loose enough for her to slip two fingers' width between it and her throat. It would allow her to breath and swallow, but she couldn't pull it off over her head.

The ceremony over, Yvette rose and went to stand with the other newly banded humans, more questions than

103

ever swirling about in her head. What did the band mean? Did it do anything? If the invaders just came last week, how did they manage to build up such a big supply of the bands so quickly? Did that mean they'd been preparing for this invasion for a long time, unbeknownst to the Empire? Of course, the way the attack had been carried out showed they'd scouted Omicron pretty thoroughly – but how had they done it without making their presence known to the humans?

There were more questions than easily available answers, so Yvette just stood silently with the group, waiting for the remainder of her fellow captives to receive their collars.

When that was accomplished, the prisoners were herded off again in another direction, this time to a lumberyard's worth of boards and timber. A few brisk gestures from the overseer made it clear their task would be to carry the lumber from its present location to where it was needed for building. It was a mindless and simple enough task, and Yvette fell to it enthusiastically, hoping the physical exertion would help rid her body of the last of the poisons from the yellow smoke so she could be fresh to confront her new situation.

An older woman in the group, though, was not up to such strenuous activity. She looked to be in her late fifties, and appeared to have some problem with her legs. She was carrying one end of a heavy load of boards across the compound when her legs gave out and she crumpled to the ground. The lumber she'd been carrying went down with her, scattering across the dirt.

The overseer was beside her immediately, exhorting her to get up, but the woman merely cried with the pain. Angrily the alien grabbed her by the arms and yanked her to her feet, which only collapsed under her again more painfully. The woman was sobbing hysterically, and work stopped around her as the prisoners stood by and watched the drama, waiting to see what would happen next.

Waiting, though, was not Yvette's style. Even though it meant some risk to herself, her instincts would not let her be a mute witness as some innocent woman was beaten and abused. Putting down her own load, she walked quickly to the side of the fallen woman. 'It'll be smooth, *gospozha*,' she whispered gently in the woman's ear. 'I'll help you up.'

She felt a hand on her shoulder as the overseer moved to push her away. Yvette looked angrily up into that green, alien face. 'I'm just helping her do her job, no thanks to you. She'll be smooth if you leave her alone.'

If the alien understood, he gave no indication of it. Instead he pushed Yvette away from the woman's body, hard enough to knock the DesPlainian to the ground herself. Yvette was a bit surprised – these little fellows were stronger than they looked. Getting back on her feet, she returned to where the overseer had started beating the fallen woman, then grabbed his arm and pushed him over backwards the same way he'd pushed her.

Out of the corner of her eye, Yvette could see a few of the alien guards converging on the spot. The last thing she'd wanted was real trouble, where they were armed and she wasn't; even with her knives, she could scarcely hope to survive such an encounter. She quickly helped the woman to her feet again and turned to face the approaching overseers with her hands spread apart from her body in what she hoped would be interpreted as a gesture of submission.

'I don't want to give you *mokoes* a hard time,' she said in a soothing tone. 'I was just helping a lady stand up. See, I'll get back in line now and everything will be smooth. No need to fire those big, nasty guns.'

If the aliens understood Empirese they gave no indication of it. Despite her soothing tone and verbal assurances, Yvette saw one of the creatures reach to his side and start to pull out an object. It was a tubular device with a handle, looking for all the world like a weapon. Although alien expressions could conceivably be different, the look on his face convinced Yvette he was going to use the device on her.

The moment for calm obeisance had passed. With her life on the line anyway, Yvette threw caution to the winds and went in to a full self-defense mode. Rather than backing away from the fight, she ran full speed at the alien who'd begun drawing his weapon. A high, well-placed kick sent the device flying from his hand. Spinning on the ball of her right foot, she came around and walloped the creature on the side of the head, knocking him to the ground. Her momentum continued to spin her around until she planted her left foot again. She was in a crouch facing two more aliens, prepared for further action.

She was not prepared, however, for what happened next. Her skirmish with the first alien, even though it had lasted just a few seconds, had given the others time to draw their own tube devices. Yvette found herself staring down two separate barrels. She tensed to spring to her right, but even her DesPlainian reflexes weren't quick enough.

Rays of energy streamed forth from the barrels of both guns, bathing the young woman in a pale yellow glow. Prepared for the searing intensity of blaster beams, Yvette's whole body tensed and a final, silent prayer flashed through her mind. These weapons were not blasters, though, and the effect of the rays was far more subtle – and in some ways, more frightening.

To Yvette, the whole world suddenly seemed detached and very far away. Her sensory apparatus was undamaged, and impulses reached her brain in the normal way,

106

but they seemed to belong to someone else, and scarcely mattered to her at all. It was as though her will had turned to jelly and her mind to mush. She, Yvette Bavol, became a disembodied entity floating beyond the trivial concerns of her corporal form.

Somewhere, buried deep within the foam padding that seemed to surround her mind, an intellectual part of her was screaming in horror. As a finely trained athlete, Yvette was used to having her mind and body function in perfect coordination; her merest thought would be instantly converted into action when she willed it so. Suddenly, her will was cut off from her body, drifting in a limbo apart. She was there, yet she wasn't, entombed in a nightmare of living hell.

The fight stopped instantly as Yvette's body stood silently in place, waiting for guidance. One of the overseers took her firmly by the arm and led her back to where she'd dropped her own load of lumber. He gestured for her to bend down and pick it up, and obediently she did so. It was all the same to her whether she stood or worked. More commands were given, and Yvette carried them out as instructed.

Deeply buried, the inner Yvette was horrified that her body would betray her this badly. She'd heard descriptions of what it was like to be under nitrobarb, and this detached feeling sounded similar. This part of her mind fought strongly against the effects of the control ray, like a bird beating hopelessly against the bars of its cage, but it was no use. A sweat broke out on her forehead from the magnitude of the internal struggle, but she could not make her body obey her. For better or worse, her will was enslaved to the whim of her alien masters.

She spent the rest of the day performing menial tasks that required little thought or coordination. After sundown, she and the other captives were escorted to a mess area where they were served some kind of disgusting stew. Yvette had to be ordered to eat, otherwise her body would have sunk into an apathetic haze. After dinner she and the others were led into one of the inflated buildings and she was assigned a sleeping pallet on the floor. Yvette lay on her back, staring up at the ceiling for hours. She was neither awake nor asleep, but in some private purgatory where thoughts crawled past too slow to catch, too distant to matter.

Long past midnight the effects of the control ray began wearing off. Sensations and emotions reached her brain once more, starting with a trickle and rapidly becoming a flood too strong for her to handle. Yvette Bavol was a strong woman, and proud of her strength. She'd faced what had seemed certain death a dozen times without blinking an eye. She'd faced capture and torture at enemy hands with not a whimper or a whine. That was her job, and she was justifiably proud of never having betrayed it.

But this loss of control hit her hardest in that very pride that normally kept her going. Even though she knew it was no fault of her own, her body had gone over to the enemy without a struggle. She had been a pawn of the alien invaders, her will totally subjected to theirs. If Jules or Pias or even the Empress had been in her gunsights and the aliens ordered her to fire, she would have gunned them down without hesitation. For a woman used to being in control of herself, the humiliation of being a mindless slave was more than she could bear.

Yvette lay on her pallet sobbing hysterically for two hours before sleep mercifully overcame her.

The slaves were awakened at dawn the next day to receive another helping of cold slop. With less than two hours of solid sleep behind her, Yvette's spirits were even lower than they'd been before. She'd done plenty of hard work in the past on very little sleep, but the degradation and humiliation of being under the control ray's influence had a draining effect on her energies. Her muscles were cramped from the cold night on a hard floor; even standing and waiting in line for food was a major effort. Only by constantly repeating within her mind who she was and what her mission was on Omicron was she able to retain any semblance of her former life and alertness. She knew that, given any chance at all, Jules would come to rescue her; she had to be ready to take advantage of her opportunity when it presented itself.

From the very start, today's activity was different from the previous day's. Yvette and a group of other captives were separated out from the general run and seated in an open-topped cart, which drove out of the regular camp. Yvette was very careful to do nothing that would call attention to herself or resemble defiance in any way; she did not want a second dose of that horrible ray. She was a quick learner, and was not about to challenge her master's supremacy again – at least not unless there was a good chance of winning.

The cart drove for a couple of kilometers over some hills along a dirt track that could only be called a 'road' out of courtesy. As they topped one crest, Yvette looked down into the valley below and let out an involuntary gasp. Nestled there in a peaceful valley, covering dozens of square kilometers, was a contingent of alien spaceships, perhaps fifty, perhaps a hundred, clustered so closely together that Yvette could not get a clear picture of them all. Their designs were strange, but judging by their size they had to be Intermediate Class or larger. Of course, the largest ships in any fleet probably couldn't land at all – but if this was even a significant fraction of the enemy's armada, it was an impressive array.

In the foreground were two more of the inflatable

buildings. One was a large structure in its own right, though dwarfed in comparison to the cluster of ships behind it; the other appeared to be a smaller storage shed. The transport cart headed down the hill toward the buildings, stopping in front of the larger one. The overseers had the humans hop quickly off the cart and march single file into the building.

Alien though these invaders may have been, certain functions do not change. Yvette could tell from the moment she walked in the door that this building was a military headquarters of some sort. The interior was partitioned off into a series of cubicles, and aliens wearing stylized uniforms of different colors were walking officiously to and fro.

There were surprisingly few of the invaders on staff in here; perhaps they had most of their work computerized, or perhaps most of the officers were supervising construction at the slave camp. Whatever the reason, this military office was ridiculously understaffed. Yvette contemplated silently how easy it would be to break in here and get whatever information was available – provided she could recognize the important information when she saw it. Right now, only Tatiana had the potential to read the alien symbols – and Yvette had no idea where the albino woman was, or even if she was still alive.

Throughout the day, Yvette and the other humans were made to fetch and tote supplies from the storage shed into the main building and up and down the central corridor of the headquarters, in and out of the various cubicles, until she knew pretty thoroughly where everything was in here. What she didn't know was how to make use of that knowledge, or how to get anything out of here if she should acquire it.

Nevertheless, as the cart drove back to the slave camp at the end of a hard day's work, Yvette was starting to feel more positive about herself and her mission once more. Despite the setbacks that had overtaken her she'd still managed to discover a key point in the aliens' defenses. There was little she could do except keep her eyes open and wait. Everything now would depend on how well Jules and the other team members managed on their own.

But if they came for her, Yvette vowed she was going to be ready. She had a personal score to settle with these green-skinned invaders.

# CHAPTER 9

## *Freedom Raid*

Realizing they had a lot of distance to cover to reach the slave camp and alien base, the Empire team spent some time looking around for a different mode of transportation. The groundcar, while comfortable, was entirely too slow and too limited to serve as a reconnaissance vehicle. After a short search they found something more to their purpose: a copterbus trapped in the ruins of an old storage shed. It may have been a part of the city's public transport system, judging from the insignia on its sides, but it had been in the shop for repairs when the aliens began their bombardment and had been overlooked in the ensuing chaos. Fortier and Ivanov, having the most complete knowledge of these devices, examined the vehicle carefully and pronounced it nearly fit to fly. A couple hours' work was all they needed to get it into working order again, and the team was off on its mission into the heart of alien territory.

Even at the copter's top speed the journey was several hours long and the five team members spent that time looking nervously out the windows on all sides, alert for any sign of enemy activity. They remembered how quickly the aliens had spotted the *H-16* when it was orbiting Omicron and they wanted to be prepared to defend themselves if they should be spotted again.

About halfway along the route to where their maps said the Long River valley was, they flew over a large town that had survived the bombing intact. On impulse Jules ordered that they stop here and pick up some supplies. 'We don't know what we'll be facing when we get there, and I'd like to be prepared for any trouble,' he reasoned, and Lady A agreed with him.

They found some food that hadn't been ransacked by marauders fleeing to the countryside, but just as importantly they came across a construction supply company. The company stocked explosives, detonators and fuses, and the team greedily loaded themselves up on those commodities. Facing an enemy with superior firepower, they would need all the explosive force they could carry to make the battle more even.

Feeling more securely armed, the group took off again toward the alien camp. They flew at an intermediate altitude that was an awkward compromise of necessity – high enough to minimize the risks of being seen or heard from the ground, but low enough, they hoped, to slip in under the watchful gaze of the alien sensors that were scanning the skies for signs of imperial retribution. They hoped to get some aerial view of the enemy's layout without being spotted themselves; if they knew what the obstacles were, they could make better plans to overcome them.

Miraculously, their luck held. The aliens, so alert for ships coming from off the planet, paid almost no heed to anything that happened on Omicron itself. It fit the pattern the group had witnessed before, a casual disdain of any defense or offense the local humans could throw against them. It was as though the aliens, having humiliated Omicron's defenses in a few short hours, no longer worried about any threat from this direction. Perhaps they were preoccupied with future plans of conquest; aside from occasional forays to obtain slaves, they gave no thought to the Omicronians whatsoever. Jules found this strange behavior, but reminded himself they were dealing with alien minds that very probably had their own unique ways of looking at the universe.

113

At any rate, he was not going to count the teeth on this particular gift horse. The Empire needed this information too badly, and he was going to get all the aliens would allow him.

At last they approached the Long River valley and Lady A, who was piloting the copter, slowed their pace so they could get a better view. As they passed over a set of low hills, they caught sight of the slave camp sprawled casually on the riverbank. Their copter was so high that the figures were little more than dots, and it was impossible to tell which were humans and which were aliens. There was a continual stream of activity, though, as the slaves seemed in the process of building a small city around the outskirts of the large temporary inflated buildings.

The late afternoon sun gleamed off some tall metal object a few kilometers away, over another set of hills. 'There's something over there,' Lady A said. 'I think we should find out what it is.' Without waiting for further discussion, she swung the copter in that direction and flew off to investigate.

In less than a minute the alien landing field came into view. The more-or-less rectangular array of ships stretched out for several kilometers across the otherwise deserted plain; it was a solemn sight, an example of the power this alien foe would bring to any fight with the Empire. 'If we assume their bigger ships are still out in space,' Fortier said, 'this is a pretty impressive little navy.'

'We also have to assume, for the moment, that this is only a small fraction of their total fleet, just enough to subdue a single planet effectively,' Lady A added. 'If their entire force is significantly larger than this, the Empire will be in serious trouble.'

Fortier could only nod silently. While he wasn't privy to the information on the exact size of the Imperial Navy, he could make a rough estimate based on the number of naval stations scattered throughout the Empire and the number of ships normally assigned to those stations. If what they saw below them was truly representational of the alien fleet, the Empire would indeed have a fight on its hands.

'There's some buildings down there,' Ivanov said, pointing to the two temporary structures, one large, one small, that stood apart near the southeast edge of the landing site near a low range of wooded hills.

Jules studied the larger building carefully. There was a steady stream of people in and out of it, and its very position this close to the ships indicated it could be of strategic importance. 'I think we may have found our target,' he said aloud.

'I agree,' Lady A said. 'A building on the edge of their landing field must have some military significance. Memorize the layout quickly; I want to get away from here before they start paying attention to us. When we're safely hidden on the ground we can discuss strategy.'

She flew off again into a wooded area in the hills a few kilometers from both the slave camp and the landing field. Setting the copter down in a clearing with just barely enough room for straight vertical takeoff and landing, she proclaimed this spot as their temporary headquarters and started right off discussing their plan of attack.

'Our target has to be that larger building by the landing field,' she said. 'Even if it isn't their military headquarters there's bound to be important information about their ships and their manpower. Tatiana, how are you coming on their language?'

'Those instruction cards were an enormous help,' the young woman replied. 'My biggest worry was that the language would have a separate ideogram for each word or concept, like ancient Chinese and Japanese. That would take months of concentrated effort and plenty of samples to figure out. Fortunately, they seem to build words out of alphabet symbols. I've got most, if not all, the symbols identified; it's just a question of building up a vocabulary and a grammar. That's an accelerating process; the more material you give me to work with, the better I'll get.'

'We may end up getting you a lot in a hurry,' Lady A told her. 'You'll have to work under pressure, possibly with a battle going on around you.'

'I understand,' Tatiana said grimly. 'I'll do the best I can.'

'What about the building itself?' Lady A asked next, looking directly at Jules.

The SOTE agent was all business. 'It's a very simple structure, an inflated long tunnel with a hemispherical cross section, one door at each end and no windows. Far too simple, really; I'd rather work on something with a lot of edges and corners, a lot of places to hide. There's no way to *sneak* into that building; we'll have to go through one door or the other, and that makes us vulnerable. Unless the building is totally deserted, we'll have to make an assault on it and capture it, at least long enough to find the information we want and get safely away again.'

Lady A nodded. 'My assessment, too. But time is short and this is the best target we've found yet. We can't help but learn something of value here. Also, we were wondering how to get off-planet again once we'd picked up our information; this would solve that problem at the same time. If we learn enough to make it worth leaving Omicron, we've got a landing field full of ships to choose from.'

The discussion about whether to penetrate this building continued for a little while, but it was mostly for completeness's sake; Jules, too, had come to the conclusion that this hut was a worthwhile target. The argument went pro and con for a few minutes to make sure no vital points had been overlooked, but once the decision had been made the discussion centered on the pivotal issue of *how* the raid would be accomplished.

'The fact is,' Jules pointed out, 'we don't know how many of the enemy are stationed inside the building at any given time.'

'Nor how many are billeted in the nearby ships, ready to help their comrades in case of trouble,' Fortier added. 'And there's no way to find out short of launching our attack.'

'There may be no way of learning those numbers,' Lady A said, 'but we can try to minimize them.'

Jules nodded. 'A diversion of some sort,' he agreed. 'It's the only way. If the aliens perceive a threat from some other direction, they'll move some of their people to counter it, leaving this building relatively unprotected. There'll probably be some defenders left back here, but it will maximize our chances of getting in safely.'

'The bigger the diversion, the better,' Ivanov said.

'And as luck would have it,' Jules said with a tight grin, 'there's a diversion-in-the-making waiting for us just over the hill.'

'The slave camp!' Tatiana exclaimed.

'Exactly. There's a few thousand humans kept there under guard, probably itching for the chance to break free. If we start enough of a ruckus over there, aliens will come running from the base camp to get things under control.'

'Or they could just decide to wipe out the entire camp with a few well-placed bombardments,' Lady A said. 'That would erase our diversion along with a few thousand innocent lives.'

'I didn't realize innocent lives meant that much to you,' Jules said. 'But I don't think they'll do that. They've gone to considerable trouble to round up their slaves and start building this city of theirs. I don't think they'd want to start over if they could help it. They'd at least make some effort to get things under control in the camp before going to the ultimate solution. If we work it right, that should be all the time we'll need.'

'And in the meantime, a diversion in the slave camp would give you the opportunity to rescue Periwinkle, wouldn't it?' Lady A asked sarcastically.

'I won't deny it,' Jules said. 'Why, is that such a terrible thing?'

'Not if we're careful to keep in mind that rescuing Periwinkle is at best only a secondary consideration,' Lady A replied. 'The real mission will be in that headquarters building. Compared to that, Periwinkle is expendable.'

Exact details of the mission were discussed and argued over for the next several hours. The sun had long since set before the team started putting their plan into operation.

They would split into two groups – one to create the diversion, the other to assault their real target. Tatiana, of course, would have to be part of the assault, since she was the only one who could tell them when they'd found what they wanted. Since the real fighting would be in the building, and since Tatiana needed to be protected at all costs, Lady A insisted that the two best people in the group should accompany the translator – namely Jules and herself. That left Fortier and Ivanov to create the diversion at the slave camp.

Their biggest problem would be coordination. It would do no good to have the diversion occur prematurely and have all the excitement be over by the time Jules and his party were in position to storm the building. Yet there was only one copter, and Fortier and Ivanov needed it to roust the slave camp. Jules, Tatiana and Lady A would have to trek overland to the landing field and then wait for the aliens to run out and defend the slave camp. Jules gave a conservative estimate of five hours for them to accomplish the trek; after that time, the other two men were to make their raid on the camp. It would still be dark then, and Jules's group could afford to wait around until the diversion started. Without radio communications between the two parties, this was the only way to handle the timing.

While Jules's party set off on their journey back to the landing site, Fortier and Ivanov had hours of time on their hands. They spent some of it fashioning the explosives they'd brought with them into crude bombs, then checked their guns and their equipment over several times. Finally, at the appointed hour, they took off in the copter back toward the slave camp.

The aliens had not bothered to light the area very much, as all the work was done in daylight and the slaves slept peacefully at night. The camp was hard to find in the dark, but the two men were aided by the light of Omicron's moon, which was in its final quarter phase. With Fortier at the controls, the copter and its small crew threw caution to the wind and swooped in low over the camp.

Ivanov played the role of bombardier, dropping their homemade explosive devices out the copter's hatch onto the ground below. The bombs hit empty patches of ground around the inflated barracks buildings, but the noise and the concussions they produced were more than satisfactory to start a panic.

Many of the people in the camp had lived through the alien bombardment of just a few days before; the horror of death raining from the skies was still fresh in their memories. At the first sounds and flashes from the exploding bombs, they sat up in their pallets, shaking with terror. As the blasts continued, wave upon wave, they panicked. Screaming in fright, they ran from the buildings. They'd seen what happened to people trapped in the rubble of falling masonry, and they wanted to be out under open skies to minimize the danger. Fear of what the aliens might do to them took second place to the emergency of the moment. Within seconds, the once quiet camp was filled with running, yelling people.

The alien response was only slightly slower. From a single building at one end of the compound, a troop of alien figures poured out like ants to defend a stepped-on nest. They had blaster-like weapons drawn, and were firing wildly into the air even before they knew what their target was, hoping that some random shot might disable their still unseen adversary.

Fortier dodged his craft in and out of the blasterfire as best he could. The copterbus was a big, lumbering vehicle, much slower to respond to controls than were the fast military copters Fortier was used to piloting; by the same token, it was heavier and more durably constructed. The aliens below were armed only with handheld blasters. A beam occasionally hit its mark but, unless some vital spot got hit, a few burns on the metal sides would not bring down the big copterbus.

Ironically, Fortier and Ivanov found themselves handicapped by their own success. They'd had their pick, at first, of places to drop their bombs, but as more and more of the captives were racing frantically around in the compound there were fewer places to safely explode a charge without hurting the very people they wanted to free. Such moral considerations probably wouldn't have stopped Ivanov if he'd been acting alone, but Fortier had made it clear to him before they started that he wanted to keep the loss of human life as low as possible. Aliens were expendable as far as he was concerned, but too many Omicronians had already died during this sad affair.

Fortunately, the sight of so many aliens pouring out of the end building gave the two men a new target to shoot for. Weaving his way through the searing beams that cut the night sky, Fortier flew the copterbus toward the enemy sanctuary. The aliens could see him coming, now, and took careful aim, but the thick commercial plating of the copter continued to serve them in good stead.

As they swooped in over the alien headquarters, Ivanov dropped a small series of bombs, each of which exploded with a satisfactory blast. Together, they brought the alien center to a state of collapse, and sent the creatures themselves into a panic nearly as complete as their captives'.

Fortier swung the craft around again and flew to the far side of the compound, where he brought the copter down to a quick landing. The vehicle had served its purpose for now; the longer it stayed in the air, the more it became a focal point for alien gunners. With so many people running around on the ground, it was actually safer to be down among them than to be a solitary target up in the air. With luck, the copter would survive to be an escape craft for them later; right now, they had more chaos to sow in the camp.

As soon as the copter had set down, even before the engines had shut off, Fortier and his comrade were out the doors, blasters in their hands and ready for trouble. It was their job to keep the confusion stirred up here at the camp long enough for their compatriots back at the landing field to accomplish their objective.

There was no doubt that they had created major confusion within the camp. People had started running around crazily during the initial panic; now that there were no more explosions, some of that panic was easing

121

and the more level-headed of them were regaining their composure. The hostility they'd had to suppress against their alien taskmasters now came boiling to the surface with a white-hot rage. Groups formed spontaneously, charging at lone aliens with little regard for their own safety. The aliens fired into the crowd, both with blasters and with the eerie beams of the mysterious controlling ray. Nothing could stop the onslaught of the humans, though, and the overseers were quickly overwhelmed.

Then, from over the hill in the direction of the landing field, reinforcements arrived. Fortier greeted the sight with mixed emotions; it would make his task here both more difficult and more dangerous, but at the same time it showed he'd accomplished his main objective – to leave the aliens' main base as deserted as possible for his companions to attack. Now that the additional aliens were here, it was his job to keep them so busy they wouldn't have the chance to go back and help at the base.

He ran quickly back into the copter and, grabbing the last of the homemade bombs, used it as a grenade and threw it at one approaching cartload of alien soldiers. A few of the creatures saw the bomb coming and jumped off the back of the cart, but most of them were caught by the explosion that followed. Fortier smiled grimly and turned back to the scene in the slave camp.

The compound was brightly lit, now, with the flickering glow of the fires set off by the bombs. In the eerie red light the camp took on a sense of unreality, as though Hierony-mus Bosch had decided to add one more scene to his view of Hell. People and strange alien creatures swarmed about, taking their toll on one another with any weapons that came to hand.

Fortier and Ivanov waded through the surging mass of humanity, firing with their blasters at any aliens they saw and killing more than a few. The compound became less crowded as more and more of the humans, seeing their chance, bolted for the hills and freedom. If the aliens wanted to reconquer their slaves, they'd have a devilishly hard time of it.

Fortier was running through the open yard when an alien suddenly appeared from around the corner of a building. The creature had its gun out, all set to fire. Fortier turned toward it and knew he would be too late. He raised his arm anyway to fire, just as the alien aimed at him.

Then a blasterbolt hit the creature from behind, and it tumbled forward lifelessly, face down in the dirt. Around the corner came Yvette, holding one of the alien guns she'd taken from a dead soldier. Tucked in her belt was one of the controlling ray tubes; it wasn't a weapon to use in a riot like this, but she'd grabbed one from a dead alien anyway. If there was no use for it later, she could take it back to Earth and have it analyzed.

Fortier gave her a smile and a brief salute. 'I guess we're even,' he said.

Yvette ran a finger around the rim of the metal slave collar she'd been forced to wear. 'Can you help me get this thing off? I hate the very thought of it.'

Fortier tried briefly to twist the collar apart, but the metal band was stubborn. 'No time now,' he said. 'It'll have to wait till we have better tools. Come on, you've loafed long enough, there's work to do.'

'You mean you didn't come just to rescue me?'

'Not officially. We're just the diversion while the others break into the headquarters over the hill.'

Yvette gave a quick nod. 'Then let's go ahead and divert, shall we?'

Now up to full complement, the team fanned out and continued its destructive progress through the camp. The compound was thinning out as more of the aliens were killed and more of the humans fled down the riverbank or over the hills to freedom. There was still one pocket of alien resistance, dug in stubbornly behind one of the collapsed inflatable buildings. It would take more firepower than the three of them had available to pry them out of that position.

Fortier looked at his watch and saw, with some surprise, that two hours had elapsed since they'd begun their raid. Anything that was going to happen at the other site would have happened by now; if Jules's team had successfully assaulted the headquarters building, they'd be established in there and might need extra help holding their position.

'Enough diversion,' he called to his comrades. 'Time for strategic withdrawal. I think we'd be of more help elsewhere.'

Slowly, then, the trio started retreating from their positions, back toward the waiting copter. The enemy soldiers sensed a change in the tempo of the fighting, and within seconds came swarming up out of their trench, charging the three retreating figures. Moving at a full run and firing back only occasionally, the Empire group raced to the copterbus. Fortier made it first and kicked the engines quickly to life. Dodging through a barrage of blasterfire, Yvette dove through the open hatch, banging her head and shoulders hard against the seat but otherwise intact.

Ivanov was a touch slower. He arrived at the copter just as Fortier was about to take off. Yvette reached back to grab his arm and pull him in when three different energy beams hit him in a crossfire. Ivanov screamed as his clothing caught fire and the beams burned holes clear through his body. His fingers stiffened momentarily in Yvette's grip, then pulled away as he fell dead at the base of the copter. Fortier, unwilling to waste any more time here, zoomed recklessly into the air and away from the charging aliens.

Yvette turned away. She'd seen people killed by blaster-fire before, had even killed a few traitors herself that way, but it was never a pretty sight. She'd just been on a killing rampage, but those had been aliens who'd killed and enslaved innocent people. This was different.

'Ivanov was a murderer and a traitor,' she said softly. 'He'd have been condemned to death by any court in the Empire.'

'I know,' Fortier said, speaking just as quietly. 'But for a while, he was a compatriot. He fought at our side and shared the risks with us to help save the Empire. It always hurts when you lose a comrade.'

Fortier had the copter make a turn and hover a second out of range of the blasters, looking back at the burning slave camp. He thought of the 'missing man' formation he'd flown too many times to honor a fallen colleague. He resolved to fly one for Ivanov as he kicked the copterbus's tail around and sped off. Right now he wanted to get back to the headquarters building before they lost any more comrades.

# CHAPTER 10

## *Jackpot*

The trek over the hills to the aliens' landing field was harder than Jules had imagined. With only the light from the last quarter moon to guide them, he and Tatiana were constantly tripping over rocks and small depressions. Only Lady A, with her artificially enhanced vision, seemed to have no problem in the dim moonlight. Adding to their difficulties was the fact that Tatiana was not in top physical shape as her two companions were, and had to pause frequently to rest. Jules fretted that they might not make it to the site before Fortier and Ivanov began their diversion.

Fortunately he'd left them plenty of time in his estimate, and the trio made it safely to the hill at the south end of the landing field well before the fireworks started in the slave camp. They looked down over the peaceful setting and began making their assault plans. 'When things start happening, they'll happen quickly,' Jules warned Tatiana. 'You'll have to go in fast with your blaster drawn, and be prepared to use it.'

'Shoot to kill,' Lady A added coldly. 'It would be nice to have prisoners to question, but we don't have the facilities for such a luxury and we don't know yet how to tell the privates from the generals. We'll have to settle for any written material we can find.'

They climbed quietly down the hill until they reached a boulder that could provide them adequate cover. While the other two waited, Jules sneaked out and planted explosive charges by the unguarded front and rear doors to the headquarters building. Then he slipped back to the hiding place and waited for the diversion to begin.

Things started happening right on schedule. Even though the slave camp was a few kilometers away, Jules heard the dull roar of the exploding bombs and he could picture the chaos that must have broken out over there. He and the others waited patiently for their plan to show effects here.

They didn't have too long to wait. A strange thrumming sound – the alien equivalent of a siren, Jules guessed – filled the air, and within seconds the base was alive with activity. Swarms of enemy soldiers came scrambling out of the building and out of some nearby ships. A loudspeaker blared some incoherent gibberish, and the soldiers ran to take their places on three open-topped carts. The carts took off into the night, over the hill to the slave camp.

Jules watched them go. He would have loved to take some shots at them – the soldiers seated there made simple targets – but he had more important things to take care of here. Those soldiers were Fortier's and Ivanov's responsibility.

They waited a few more minutes to make sure no more aliens would be leaving the area. When they were certain the situation had stabilized, Jules gave a silent nod and the trio moved out of hiding and down toward their predetermined positions. Lady A waited by the door to the far end of the building; Jules kept Tatiana with him for safety's sake at the near end.

When he could see that Lady A was set at her end, Jules touched the control that detonated the first set of explosives in front of his door. The blast shattered the simple wood construction, opening a gaping hole for him to enter.

'Stay behind me,' he called to Tatiana as he leaped through the cloud of dust and smoke left in the wake of the explosion. Actually, he moved so quickly that the young woman would have been hard pressed to do anything else. Her main concern was staying out of his way while he was in action.

Only a small contingent of aliens had been left behind to guard this building; the main threat was thought to be at the slave camp. Although all of them were armed, the nearest ones had no time to draw their weapons before the deadly beams from Jules's blaster cut them down. By the time the creatures at the far end of the building could start firing back, Jules and Tatiana were well inside the building and safely behind the cover of a partition.

Then, to add to the enemy's confusion, the Empire team initiated stage two of their assault. The second explosive charge was detonated outside the far door and Lady A came racing into the building like an avenging Fury, her blaster carving a swath through the alien forces.

This assault from two directions at once totally demoralized the enemy soldiers. Lady A was a blur to the eyes, a literally inhuman killing machine; even Jules, no slouch himself when it came to personal combat, was impressed by the speed of her reactions and the accuracy of her aim. It put any DesPlainian to shame, and he was glad she was on his side, however temporarily.

Caught in a crossfire between Jules and Lady A, the aliens had no chance at all. Within minutes the opposition lay dead on the ground: Jules, Tatiana and Lady A found themselves in sole possession of the aliens' headquarters.

'Now comes the hard part,' Lady A said casually, as though killing a few dozen creatures were no more a task than brushing her teeth. 'We have to look through this entire building and find something of value, to make all this carnage worth the effort.'

This task would fall almost entirely on Tatiana's shoulders; it was her reason for being along on the mission in the first place. The desks in the various cubicles were all computerized, as would have been expected in a human office, but nonetheless their tops were cluttered with paper and printed cards much like the instruction cards they'd found in the ruins of the walking tower.

Tatiana started reading these at random. Her purpose was twofold. First, she was trying to build up a vocabulary and grammar by guessing at the meaning of new words through their context with ones she already knew. Second, she was looking for key words or phrases that would indicate a document of special importance. There had to be something in all this vast array of information that would tell them about the aliens, their background, and their plans for the future.

Jules and Lady A were unable to read the alien language, but they did not stand idly by. They had to be constantly on the alert for any more soldiers re-entering the building so they could protect Tatiana and give her as much time as possible to do her job. They also moved through the building on their own looking for signs they themselves could interpret, such as a larger or more impressive looking office which might belong to a more important officer. The odds of finding something valuable were higher there than on the desks of junior level staff.

As Jules was rummaging through one cubicle, he pushed aside the dead body of one of the aliens. As it fell to the ground he noticed something strange, and bent over to examine it more closely.

The creature had died from a blaster beam; the burn hole in its uniform and the charred flesh on its chest attested to that. Yet, strangely, there was no blood. Blaster wounds were often known to cauterize themselves by the nature of the energy beam, but it was seldom a perfect seal; there was usually some leakage of blood or lymph from the burn. Here there was nothing and, thinking back on it, Jules could not recall seeing blood from any of the bodies.

He became aware of Lady A standing over him with a looming presence. 'Have you taken up xenobiology as a hobby?' she asked icily.

'They don't bleed,' Jules pointed out, ignoring her sarcasm. 'There's not a drop of blood anywhere.'

The woman knelt beside him and glanced at the corpse. 'You're right,' she said. 'A curious phenomenon. We'll have to mention that in our report when we get back; perhaps the experts can make something of it. Maybe their wounds cauterize better than ours, or maybe they don't have a circulatory system the way humans do.'

She stood up again. 'It's pointless for us to speculate, since neither of us is an expert on comparative anatomy. And while it's true that any information we gather is important at this stage, I think we'd do better looking for military rather than scientific data. If this does become an all-out war, there'll be plenty of corpses for the scientists to dissect later.'

She was probably right, Jules conceded as he himself straightened up and continued on his search. Nevertheless, the curious part of his mind that was always turning over strange facts and oddly shaped pieces of information refused to let go of this particular tidbit. Something was tickling his brain, telling him that this might be an important clue to the secret of the aliens. If only he knew how to interpret it correctly. But when no instant enlightenment came he filed the fact in the back of his mind, to let his subconscious play with it at its leisure.

A few minutes later he came to one cubicle near the center of the building that felt important. There was no particular factor he could point to; the cubicle may have been slightly larger than most of the others, the desk of a richer looking wood, the chair a bit bigger, but in themselves those were trivial concerns. Something about the arrangement of the office, though, gave him the firm impression that someone of importance had been stationed here. He called Lady A over to see how she would react to it.

Her instincts corroborated his own. 'I think we should do some serious looking in here,' she agreed. 'Tatiana, if you don't have something else important right now, come and try some of these things.'

The albino woman came over and began sifting through the papers on top of the desk. During even the brief time she'd had to study so far, her computer-assisted memory had enabled her to attain a reasonable level of proficiency with the alien language, so she could skim rapidly through the papers, putting aside ones that were of an obviously trivial nature.

As she was glancing over the material, a handful of alien soldiers burst into the building from outside. Jules didn't know whether they came from the ships or whether they'd circled back from the fracas at the slave camp, but they had to be dealt with if Tatiana was to continue her work. He and Lady A fought furiously for the next several minutes while Tatiana tried to ignore them and continue reading. By the time the aliens were eliminated and the other two returned to her side, Tatiana was looking very excited.

'I think I've found something,' she said, holding up a series of cards. 'It's a list of some sort with several columns, and it goes on for pages. There's a string of names in the first column, with serial numbers and a string of classification figures in the others.'

'It could just be a personnel roster,' Lady A said.

Tatiana shook her head. 'I don't think so. See this symbol? It's a unit of weight. I don't know exactly how it compares to kilos, but according to the instruction manuals we found earlier one of those walking towers weighs about seven of these units. Whatever these things are on the list, they weigh between a couple dozen and several hundred of those units. Here's a few over a thousand. Those would have to be pretty heavy soldiers.'

'Ships,' Jules said.

Lady A nodded. 'It would appear that way.' She took the lists from Tatiana's hands and gave them a quick skim. 'There's well over a thousand listings here, so this can't be just a roster of their ships on Omicron. It may be a partial or complete listing of their entire fleet.'

She tucked the cards into an interior pocket of her bodysuit. 'We don't have to do a detailed analysis now; we can leave that to the experts when we get back. It's enough to know it's something of importance. Keep looking, there's got to be more treasure around here.'

Encouraged by her success, Tatiana approached her task with renewed vigor. Within a couple of minutes she'd made another discovery. 'Looks like a series of star maps,' she said. 'And here's a list of coordinates. I'm not sure how they relate to our own coordinate system . . .'

'Any competent astronomer can figure that out,' Lady A said impatiently. 'We'll take those along with us, too.'

'It's a good bet nearly everything on this desk is of some value,' Jules said. 'We can't take the whole thing with us. I've got a better idea. Spread those cards and papers out on the desktop, face up.'

As Tatiana complied with his instructions, Jules reached into the utility pouch at his waist and took out a miniature camera. He began snapping pictures at a furious rate. 'This also has the advantage,' he commented as he worked, 'that we leave the originals behind, so the enemy won't be sure how much information we got from them. The more confusion the better.'

Lady A said nothing, but Jules noticed she was looking over his shoulder and staring intently at the documents spread out on the desktop. He reminded himself once

132

more that, despite her body's perfectly human appearance, she was really a remarkably clever machine. She was stronger and faster than any human being, and she could see quite clearly in almost no light at all. There was no reason to suppose she didn't have a photographic memory system built into her as well. He hardly expected her to tell him the intimate details of her construction, but he was willing to bet she was also photographing these papers for redundancy.

He said nothing about his suspicions aloud, but continued photographing all the documents in a professional manner. When he finished, he replaced the material approximately where they'd found it, so the aliens would have a hard time knowing what they'd seen and what they hadn't.

'A high-ranking officer usually surrounds himself with his top aides,' Lady A said. 'The desks immediately around here might also have important information. Tatiana, can you make a quick check?'

The young woman hastened to comply. The very next desk was virtually devoid of any written material, but the one beyond that was filled with the printed cards that seemed to be the aliens' favorite publishing format. Tatiana leafed through them quickly, until she came to some that caused her to slow down.

'I think I've really found something here,' she said quietly. 'It's a list of some of those same ship names with coordinates and dates. It's talking about large-scale coordination and logistics.'

'It might just be a list of past military maneuvers,' Lady A said.

'Most of the verbs are in future tense,' Tatiana insisted. 'If I had to bet money, I'd say these are future plans of some sort.'

Jules needed no further encouragement, and began

taking pictures of these documents as well. Lady A repeated her action of looking over his shoulder while he was doing the photography, increasing his suspicion that she was also recording the information for her own use. Jules didn't see any harm in that, as long as the Empire also had a copy – but he would make sure his camera and its electronic recordings were delivered intact to the Head.

He'd just finished the photography and was putting the cards away again when Lady A straightened up. 'We've got company coming,' she said in calm but urgent tones.

Jules made a mental note that her hearing must be extra sensitive as well; he hadn't heard anything yet, and he was usually pretty good at detecting such things. He began almost to envy her advantages. Nevertheless, he took her word for it and pulled out his blaster. Lady A and Tatiana did the same, and the three took defensive positions where they could cover the doors at either end of the building.

A few seconds later, squads of alien soldiers burst into the building from both ends, and the air was quickly filled with the light and heat of blasterbolts. The fierce energies involved charged the very atmosphere, leaving the strong smell of ozone characteristic of prolonged blaster battles.

Jules, Tatiana and Lady A were pinned in a crossfire near the center of the long building. In the initial exchange of fire they managed to hit a few of the aliens before the enemy was able to dig in to positions of their own. The green-skinned soldiers kept pouring energy into the center at a prodigious rate, hoping to burn their opponents out into the open. A few of the nearby desks caught fire, and the flames threatened to spread to the partitions between the offices, giving the Empire team fewer objects to hide behind safely.

Jules looked around. This would be the ideal time for a

retreat, but the aliens had both the doors covered. The building had no windows, but the walls appeared to be of a plastic fabric that was open to suggestions. *When there aren't any exits, make your own,* Jules thought in desperation.

Turning, he directed his blaster's energy behind him instead of at the enemy soldiers. The plastic fabric was amazingly tough, but eventually it yielded to the heat of the beam trained on it. Within a couple of minutes Jules had cut a gash wide enough for the three humans to slip through. Lady A had watched what he was doing and said nothing disapproving, so Jules assumed she agreed with his idea.

'Let's go!' he cried when the hole was big enough and, taking the lead, he raced through the newly created slot in the building's wall. The edges of the fabric were still glowing from the heat of his beam, but he was through the hole and out into the darkness of night before he had much chance to feel it. Behind him, Tatiana and Lady A made the same dash for freedom through the slot he'd carved.

After the exchange of blaster beams and the fires spreading through the building, the night air felt wonderfully cool against Jules's skin. There was little time to enjoy the sensation, though; the aliens were pouring out the doors again, trying to get a clear shot at them in the open. Jules raced up the hill to a spot behind the boulder where they'd waited before the raid. Behind him, Tatiana tripped but Lady A swept the young woman up in her arms as though she were scarcely heavier than a pillow and carried her at top speed to the hiding place beside Jules. The head of the conspiracy was not about to lose her special translator at this stage of the game.

They'd made it out of one trap, but their position was not much better here. They had more room to retreat up the hill behind them if they chose, but the aliens still outnumbered them and would be coming in pursuit if they fled. Lady A might be able to go on forever, but Jules knew there were limits even to his DesPlainian endurance. Those limits would be reached quickly if he had to run uphill away from followers determined to kill him.

As his mind was sorting out various alternatives, a new factor entered the picture. Swooping down from the sky like a silent avenger came the copterbus, piloted by Captain Fortier. The craft zoomed recklessly toward one group of the aliens clustered at the near door of the building, cruising just a couple of meters above the ground and forcing the creatures to take cover. From out of the copter's passenger hatch came a blaster beam that cut down several of the soldiers. Jules gave a whoop of triumph at the sudden reappearance of their allies. Lady A looked at him with distaste, but at this moment he didn't care whether she thought him childishly emotional. He was happy to see his comrades, especially now.

The copterbus zoomed parallel to the side of the building, buzzing the aliens who'd come out of the other door, temporarily forcing them back inside. With the area momentarily cleared of fighting, the copter slued around and landed right in front of the boulder where the three fugitives were hiding. The passenger door opened invitingly.

Jules and the others did not need further prompting. Racing out from behind their cover, they ducked below the rapidly swirling copter blades and clambered awkwardly into the waiting craft. Jules and Lady A helped Tatiana in first, then scrambled aboard themselves. Fortier barely waited for them to be inside before making a rapid vertical ascent.

The aliens came streaming out of the building again, firing at the retreating copter to no avail as the craft flew off into the nighttime sky.

136

# CHAPTER 11

## *Escape from Omicron*

Jules quickly scanned the copter's cabin and, to his delighted surprise, saw a scuffed and tired looking Yvette seated beside Fortier. He gave her a broad smile and a clenched fist sign for victory, which she acknowledged with a brief nod and a smile of her own. No words needed to be spoken; the bond between brother and sister was so strong it bordered, at times, on telepathy.

Lady A had also been checking on the cabin's occupants. 'Where's Ivanov?' she asked.

'He didn't make it out,' Fortier said in neutral tones.

'But you *did* manage to rescue Periwinkle.' Lady A's voice made the simple statement sound like an accusation.

'The two incidents were not related,' Fortier said in a coolly military manner. 'Ivanov didn't lose his life saving hers.'

'I didn't think he'd be that foolish,' was Lady A's comment, letting it be known that the subject was now closed.

After a moment's awkward silence, Fortier asked, '*Khorosho*, where do we go from here?'

'I think we've got all the information we can expect on this mission,' Lady A said. 'The enemy certainly knows we're here and will keep everything well hidden from now on. We'd best get back to Earth while we still can.'

Yvette and Fortier looked over to Jules. While Lady A's opinions were certainly important, they'd already voted Jules team leader; it would have to be his decision whether they stayed or left.

Jules considered the matter. The problem was that he

didn't know for sure just how much information they'd actually gotten. Tatiana had some hints that these documents were important, and right now she was the only expert they had. He had to take her word for some things. Still, she hadn't read any of those documents in their entirety. No matter how promising they looked, they could end up being mere dross. He and Yvette had a certain reputation for bringing in important, reliable information. He'd hate to bring these documents back to the Head, only to have them turn out worthless.

On the other hand, Lady A was right. The aliens had been alerted that a spy team was on Omicron and was after military information. If there were any other bases on Omicron housing important data, they would be tightly guarded from now on. This small team, as poorly equipped as it was, would not easily penetrate those defences. Looked at from that standpoint, it was a miracle they'd accomplished as much as they had. Any more assaults like tonight's would certainly result in more deaths on the team, with no guarantee of any further results.

Besides, even if the documents he'd photographed were totally useless, the mission could not be called a failure. They'd learned that the invaders were definitely alien beings, and they'd learned a little about their language and military strategy. They'd seen the alien weapons in operation and, if they escaped at all, it would be on board an alien ship – which would give the experts even more of an insight into the enemy's technology and method of thinking. All this was infinitely more than the Empire had when it dispatched the team to Omicron.

'She's right,' he said aloud. 'We've got all we can get. Let's leave while there's any chance at all.'

Fortier nodded and flew the copterbus high over the dark landing field, giving them a clear panorama of the possibilities. 'We've got a wide selection to choose from,' he commented.

Lady A, who had the best night vision, leaned forward and studied the field from the front window. 'We want something big enough for the five of us,' she said, 'but not too cumbersome. Speed is most important now. We'll have to get away, and you can be sure they'll try to stop us.'

After a brief conference, they decided on one scout-sized ship near the north end of the field with its main hatch ajar. Once again they would have to bet the success of the mission on Tatiana's linguistic talents. The layout and controls of the alien ship would be different than they were used to in human vessels, and Tatiana would have to tell them where the various controls were, how they were calibrated, and how they were meant to operate. And they would have to assimilate all this knowledge in record time if they were to make their getaway.

Reaching the ship of their choice, though, proved a little more difficult than they'd hoped. As their copterbus descended toward the landing field, a set of floodlights came on to illuminate the area as bright as daytime. Heavy-duty blasters mounted around the perimeter of the field began firing at the small craft, and Fortier suddenly had to do some fancy piloting to steer his way through the obstacle course of energy beams. A few of the deadly rays hit their mark, and the copterbus rocked with the impact those beams had on the metal plating of its hull.

In a desperate maneuver, Fortier sent the copter on a steep dive, plummeting between the rows of silently standing starships. Once they got below a certain angle the heavy-duty blasters could no longer fire at them for fear of hitting their own ships. There were still likely to be ground troops shooting at them, but the big artillery was silenced – at least for the moment.

Fortier threaded a course through the maze of ships until they reached the one they'd selected for their escape. The copter hit ground with an ungentle bump, and its passengers scrambled out the hatches on either side. Yvette and Lady A took the lead up the ladder into the alien scoutship, with Jules and Fortier helping Tatiana bring up the rear. By unspoken agreement the two women in front split up once they got inside the hatch, Lady A moving gun in hand toward the front of the ship and Yvette moving to the rear. They encountered no alien soldiers stationed aboard the ship, and came back to give the all- clear signal to the rest of the party. The other three hurriedly joined them.

They went immediately to the bridge, where Tatiana set about the crucial task of interpreting the ship's controls. The control room was arranged in a heptagonal shape, with seven acceleration couches facing one to each side. The couches would be cramped for human-sized passengers, even DesPlainians, but they would have to do.

As they waited for Tatiana to decipher the control boards, Jules went up to his sister and put a hand on her shoulder. 'I've got to go back out in the copter again.'

'Why?' Yvette asked, startled.

'I counted four batteries of heavy-duties spaced around the edge of the landing field. With all of them intact, we'll never be able to take off; the instant we do, they'll get us in a crossfire that'll blow us out of the sky. Someone has to put them out of commission. How many minigrenades do you have in your belt?'

'Two,' Yvette said grimly.

'With my two, that should give us just enough.' He took the grenades Yvette handed him and turned to find Fortier blocking his way.

'I'll go with you,' the naval officer said.

'No,' Jules's voice was firm. 'This is a one-person mission, and as team leader I pick the person to do it. With the exception of Lady A, I'm the best pilot with the quickest reflexes, and you'll need her to operate the ship. I won't risk a second life needlessly. Either I can do the job by myself or the copter will be shot down whether there's one person in it or two. You stay here and back up Lady A.'

He turned once more to Yvette. 'If I don't come back, make sure the Head gets this,' he said, handing her the miniature camera he'd used to photograph the enemy plans.

Their eyes locked on one another for the briefest of moments. Brother and sister had faced death so many times in the past that goodbyes had long since been said. They were aware that any parting might well be their last, and they knew the bond they had formed between them would survive the death of either. Still, there was always the wistful moment when the inevitable seemed a little closer than usual, and they paused to memorize each other's face one last time.

Then the moment passed and Jules was back to business. 'I'll make a sweep of the perimeter and knock out as many of the batteries as I can. That should give you time to learn the controls well enough to get airborne. *Don't wait around for me*. If you master the controls before I'm back, take off without me. If I get stranded down here, I'll go back to one of the cities and join the freedom fighters until the situation is resolved. The war won't last forever; I'll be smooth in the meantime.'

Yvette gave a brief nod. She didn't want him to go – she would rather have gone herself – but she understood the need for the mission. Jules would make sure their ship could take off and carry the vital information they'd acquired back to the Empire for analysis and evaluation. Yvette also knew her brother was a survivor; even if they had to abandon him here on Omicron, he'd find some way to turn the situation to advantage. In fact, knowing him, he'd probably rally the local forces into defeating the aliens and pushing them off the planet.

Then Jules was gone, and she heard the outer airlock sighing shut behind him. He was cut off, now, from all contact with them; they couldn't even see what progress he was making on his task of wiping out the enemy gun positions. They would have to trust to his abilities to do the job for them – otherwise, their escape from this world would be very short-lived.

Tatiana had started deciphering the words and numbers on the various control mechanisms. She was not a pilot herself, and could only give literal interpretations; Fortier and Lady A listened intently to every word, trying to extrapolate from what she said to what they knew had to be the case if the ship were to function.

Yvette was left without anything to do. She chafed at the uncomfortable metal slave collar as she studied the controls of some of the less important panels, trying to evaluate their purpose. If the alien creatures were logical and if form did indeed follow function, then she might be able to make some educated guesses of her own about how things worked. She wouldn't trust herself to fly the ship, but she might get some of the backup systems, like weapons or sensors, to operate.

After a few minutes of intense concentration and a couple of failures, she met with eventual success. Pressing a series of opaque plastic areas on one control board caused a visiscreen to light up, showing a scene outside one portion of the ship. Encouraged by her success, Yvette went around the room turning on all the visiscreens. Because this was a scoutship and seeing was one of its primary functions, she ended up with a complete panorama of the field around the ship – and, not incidentally, this enabled her to watch her brother's progress on his own mission.

On the north side of the ship, an area of flames showed where Jules must have been successful in his attempt to bomb the heavy-duty blasters installed there. With a bit of effort, she picked out the speck on the screen that must have been his copter, flying around to the east. Beams were shooting past him, both from the mounted weapons and from handheld blasters fired by alien soldiers, but Jules's superb reflexes – even on the sluggish controls of the copterbus – enabled him to dart through the beams with seemingly effortless abandon.

As Yvette watched, the copter made a short bombing dive at the gun emplacement on the east side of the landing field, then just as suddenly swooped up again. She couldn't see the grenade fall at this distance, but she easily saw the repercussions as a massive explosion flared on the screen. With each successive hit, the copter had less blasterfire to elude, increasing its chances of further success.

Lady A's voice broke into the stream of Yvette's thoughts. 'We think we've got the important controls figured out. Strap yourself in.'

Yvette's heart sank. Despite her brother's brave words, she didn't want to abandon him here if she could help it. 'He's only knocked out two of the gun batteries so far,' she pointed out. 'We ought to wait and see if he can get them all. It would improve our chances of taking off.'

Lady A hesitated just a fraction of a second. 'We've got to wait a few minutes for the engines to charge up, anyway. We can give him that long.' She was being uncharacteristically generous, but Yvette was willing to accept the favor.

On the screen, Jules's copter was flying steadily along on its mission, and Yvette's hopes rose that he'd complete

143

it successfully and return before they took off. But then, in a single moment, those hopes were shattered. A bolt from one of the heavy-duty blasters at the southern side of the field struck the tail rotor of the copterbus, practically severing the entire back end.

The aircraft veered crazily out of control, and Yvette held her breath. Then, with one last suicidal plunge, the copter dove directly at the gun emplacement. There was an enormous explosion as the copter and the blaster that wounded it both went up in a single ball of bright orange flames.

Yvette sat quietly in her acceleration couch, hardly daring to breathe. The image stayed etched in her memory like a frame of film frozen on a screen. Part of her didn't want to believe what she'd all too convincingly seen. It was one thing for the mind to accept intellectually the death of a close relative, and quite another to live through the experience.

From the master control console, Lady A said calmly, 'That's that. He knocked out three of the four batteries. We'll have to take our chances with the other one. Tatiana found the deflector shields, so it might not be too bad.'

Her voice was so matter-of-fact that Yvette wanted to kill her more than she'd ever wanted to in the past. At the same time, Yvette's body felt so totally limp that she'd have been utterly incapable of following through on the impulse.

If Lady A noticed Yvette's mood, she paid it no heed, turning instead to the vital task of getting the ship into the air. The engines trembled beneath them as her fingers manipulated the alien controls with careful deliberation. Then, with a mighty surge that startled all of them, the scoutship lifted off the ground in a sudden leap for the open sky.

The one remaining blaster battery tried valiantly to

shoot down the fugitive vessel. Searing beams of energy scored the sides of the ship, but the defensive shields held against the flux. In a matter of a few seconds the escaping vessel was beyond the range of the gun emplacement, soaring through the atmosphere and beyond, into the empty space surrounding the planet Omicron. Jules's final mission had been a success; he'd knocked out enough of the aliens' artillery to enable the ship to leave the planet.

But even though they were off the ground, they were still not out of danger. There were alien ships in orbit around Omicron, acting as sentries, and they began to converge on the tiny scoutship almost as soon as it cleared the atmosphere. The Empire team faced one final test of their abilities before they'd be allowed a safe escape.

Fortier and Tatiana were hastily conferring over one instrument panel, trying to figure out how the weapons system worked while Lady A grimly set about working the unfamiliar controls to steer an evasive course until they were far enough from Omicron's gravity to slip into subspace. Yvette bestirred herself to leave her seat and join Fortier and Tatiana. She couldn't help Lady A pilot the vessel and she couldn't go backwards in time to save her brother's life, but she could at least have some part in making sure the mission succeeded and Jules's death was not in vain.

As it turned out, the scoutship's weapon system was completely automated, with all aiming and firing done by computer systems. Once they figured out how to turn the systems on, the ship's computer did the rest of the job, at least as accurately as most live gunners would have been able to do. If she'd been completely familiar with the controls, Yvette might have had a slight edge – but as it was, an automated system was by far the best choice.

Slowly but surely Lady A was getting the feel of the controls. As the sentry ships closed in on the escaping vessel, she was able to start evasive actions, dodging randomly by way of the attitude controls and steering a safe course between the rays of enemy fire. The one thing that remained constant was maximum outward acceleration. They had to get away from Omicron as quickly as possible, before the enemy could mount a full-scale pursuit. The aliens had worked too hard to keep the Empire as ignorant of their existence as they could; they would not want any information leaking out before they were ready.

Realizing the importance of stopping the fugitives, a couple of the sentry ships did not bother shooting. Instead, they put all their effort into making a suicidal charge at the escaping ship with the full intention of either pulling up close enough to fire point-blank or else colliding with the scoutship and destroying it that way. The astrogational computer at the front console displayed the orbital tracks of the suicide ships as they converged toward the fugitives. The screen also displayed the locus of points far enough from Omicron to make a safe jump into subspace. The two courses intersected almost perfectly; it would be a very close escape, if they managed it.

Lady A made no attempt to avoid the confrontation with the oncoming ships. She was gambling that either her own vessel would reach the subspace point first, or else the automatic gunners would inflict severe enough damage on the approaching craft that they would be no threat. In any event, she dared not slow up lest the other pursuing sentry ships start gaining on them.

The lines on the computer screen drew closer and closer together with each passing second as suspense mounted within the cabin. Fortier, Yvette and Tatiana could do nothing but watch the screens and hope. Their fate was out of their hands; everything rested on the ability of Lady A, the alien pilots, and on the inexorable laws of physics.

146

As the suicide ships came within range, the scoutship's guns opened fire on these new targets. For a while, nothing happened. Then one of the beams scored a victory. The first of the suicide ships took a direct hit along the flank, and began careening through space out of control, no longer a threat. Undeterred, the second ship kept on coming, its path set to intersect theirs within a matter of seconds.

Yvette looked to the visiscreens, which were still turned on. At first all she could see was the darkness of space, a sprinkling of stars, and the rapidly receding image of Omicron behind them. Then, in an instant, the chase ship appeared. Because of the great relative speeds involved, it seemed to come out of nowhere heading directly at them. There was barely time for Yvette to draw an intake of breath and brace for the inevitable collision.

And then they were in subspace, and the entire picture changed. Gone were the pursuing ships and their energy beams trying to catch the scoutship in a deadly crossfire. Gone was the small craft that had tried to ram them and had come so close to succeeding. Instead, the computer screen showed a clear region around them; the local area of subspace was devoid of any ships but their own.

The situation would not stay that way for long; the aliens knew that keeping their secrecy was too important to their cause to let the scoutship get away. More and more of the pursuing vessels also dropped into the strange void of subspace the instant they were far enough from Omicron's mass to do so safely. Space battles were impossible in subspace; the laws of physics did not permit one ship to touch or contact another, although they could track and see where each was. But the aliens were not about to give up the chase. Their hope was to track the Empire team's ship until it re-emerged in normal space, at which point they would try to encircle and destroy it before the spies on board could get their information back to Earth.

For the next hour and a half, Lady A sat in front of the alien control board playing a desperate game of cat-and-mouse. At random intervals she would drop out of subspace, thereby vanishing from the aliens' detectors, hoping they would overshoot before they, too, could return to normal space and look for her ship. Then she would return to subspace and hope to speed away before they could react again.

These were standard tactics for a ship fleeing a superior force, and the aliens were prepared for it. They were not, however, prepared for the speed at which Lady A could react. Her mechanical nervous system had far faster reflexes than those of biological creatures, and in the end that factor proved decisive. More and more of the enemy ships dropped out of the chase as they were unable to keep track of the constant changes, until finally the scoutship found itself alone in subspace with no barriers between itself and an effortless journey back to the Empire.

Lady A turned back toward the others. Her perfect features were marred by neither tension nor sweat. She did not even wear the look of relief the others felt. 'Barring any unforeseen catastrophes, our mission is successfully completed,' she said calmly. 'You may congratulate yourselves on a job well done. We escaped with only thirty-three and a third percent casualties, which is actually far better than I anticipated. I expected fifty percent at least.'

Once again Yvette had to squelch the silent rage welling up inside her at the cavalier treatment of Jules's death. Their mission may indeed have accomplished its goals, but losing her beloved brother made it something less than a triumph.

# CHAPTER 12

## Plans and Alliances

The scoutship returned to Luna Base, where the members of the team became the center of the most frantic activity in the history of mankind.

Fortier, Yvette and Lady A were all thoroughly interrogated and debriefed by hordes of military experts, prying for every tiny bit of information they might possess. No detail was too insignificant, because it was impossible to say what trivial-seeming clue might offer major insight into the nature of the enemy and his plans.

The scoutship and the weapons Yvette had grabbed from a dead alien were taken to a special hangar along with her metal slave collar, and their components were analyzed. Did the aliens have any technological secrets the Empire could use? Did their ships and their weapons work on the same principles? Did they have the same range and accuracy? If a war was going to be fought, as seemed inevitable, these were questions that had to be answered. The tapes made could be measured in kilometers.

Tatiana, meanwhile, was taken aside and grilled separately. She lectured a roomful of top Empire cryptographers and linguists on everything she'd learned about the aliens' written language and the few spoken words she'd heard blared from loudspeakers at the headquarters or shouted by the attacking soldiers. They questioned her endlessly on seemingly arcane points of grammar and she answered as best she could based on the context in which she'd seen the various symbols used.

It was the documents, though, that were the real success

of the mission. Even while Tatiana was teaching the scholars the basics of the alien tongue, other experts were analyzing the captured writings to seek out any important information about the enemy's military capabilities and plans. As the contents of two desks had been photographed in toto, there was a lot of trivial information to be sorted through – but even this was not wasted, for it helped the linguists build their knowledge of the alien vocabulary and grammar. Words that were obscure in important documents became clear when examined in everyday contexts.

The informational content of the major documents, though, was so important it made the entire effort worthwhile. It included not only star maps of the aliens' home territory, but inventories of their major fleet and equipment, plus tentative plans for the invasion of the Empire of Earth. The espionage team could scarcely have found more vital data if they'd known precisely where to look.

Three days after the team's return, Zander von Wilmenhorst flew to Moscow to brief Empress Stanley Eleven personally on everything they'd uncovered. The meeting took place in the Imperial Council Chamber, a somber room that befitted such somber tidings. The heavy gold and brown velvet tapestries dampened sounds even before they reached the soundproofed walls. The leather-topped oval conference table dominated the room, but the oversized leather chairs around it were mostly empty. Because of the highly secret nature of the briefing, the only people present were the Empress, the Head, and Lord Admiral Cesare Benevenuto.

'The aliens call themselves the Gastaadi – at least, we think that's how it should be pronounced,' the Head began. 'We're a bit weak on their spoken language. They've got a sizeable little empire of their own located in toward the galactic hub – something like nine hundred planets, if we read the figures correctly.'

The Empress did a quick check on her wrist computer, the only jewelry, other than the imperial crest ring she always wore, on the deep blue uniform she'd donned for a decoration ceremony earlier in the day. 'That's only about sixty percent the size of ours.'

'True,' Benevenuto said. 'But when we're talking about numbers like that, such comparisons mean little. If it comes to all-out war, for instance, we'll have more volume to defend. We're far more spread out, while their worlds are in a more compact arrangement. Both sides have such vast resources to draw on that a protracted war could last for decades.'

'That doesn't sound promising,' Edna Stanley muttered.

'I'm in the business of doing, not promising,' her admiral told her. 'I try to deal with the facts, not beautify them.'

'How could they know so much about us when we didn't even know they existed until a couple of weeks ago?' Edna asked.

'We've lost a number of scoutships in that region of space over the last few years,' von Wilmenhorst told her. 'We didn't think anything of it at the time; finding new worlds is a highly risky business, and scoutships are lost all the time. But now that we knew what to look for, we ran a correlation check through the Primary Computer Complex and discovered that far more of our ships were being lost in that direction than anywhere else. The Gastaadi must have been capturing our people and interrogating them to find out about our capabilities. I don't know how they managed to do such thorough reconnaissance work on Omicron without being discovered – but with our not even suspecting they existed, they probably had an easier time of it than I'd like to imagine.

'Technologically, they seem about on a par with us.

151

They do some things differently than we do, but we could do the same things if we chose. Their ships operate on the same subspace principles, they use energy weapons similar to our blasters, and so forth. We're ahead of them on a couple of minor points – we build bigger and faster ships, and our blasters have better range – but they have two things we don't. For one thing, they seem to have some device that jams subcom transmissions on a planet-wide scale; there's no reference to it in the documents we captured, but that's the only explanation I can think of for how they managed to blanket Omicron so completely after the invasion began. For another, they've got a device that seems to enslave the human will; our scientists are looking it over now. It worked on no less a subject than Agent Periwinkle, and if it works on her it'll work on anyone.'

The Empress shuddered. She knew Yvette Bavol's strength of will only too well. If there was a device that could subjugate *her*, it was a frightening concept indeed.

Lord Admiral Benevenuto picked up the narrative thread when von Wilmenhorst paused for breath. 'Despite the smaller size of their empire, the Gastaadi have a larger fleet than ours. They seem to be of a more militaristic bent than we are, and they translate everything into military terms. As Zander said, our ships are a little better equipped which may compensate a bit for their larger numbers, but not much. We saw what they were willing to do to Omicron; they're aggressive, ruthless fighters convinced that force is everything. If they have their way, what happened on Omicron will be the pattern they'll set for the rest of the Empire.'

'How can we be sure of that?' the Empress asked. 'I'm not doubting what they did on Omicron, but they had a specific reason for being so thorough there – they wanted to maintain as much secrecy about themselves as possible.

Now that their secrecy is blown, perhaps they won't be as oppressive.'

Von Wilmenhorst shook his head sadly. 'Not from what our experts have been able to deduce about the Gastaadi nature. They seem to respect power and nothing else. After conquering Omicron, they showed complete disdain for the survivors. They gave almost no consideration to the possibility that anyone would fight back, and took few security precautions. That worked in our favor, or our reconnaissance team wouldn't have been as successful as it was – but it does mean they show almost no concern for the innocent victims of their aggression. Any planet that falls into their hands will be a hellhole in a matter of days. Their plans indicate they intend to move soon against more Empire worlds.'

'Yes, I understand we captured some of their plans. What exactly is going to happen?'

Benevenuto cleared his throat. 'According to what we saw, their entire fleet has been massing for the past month. Omicron was just a test case, their equivalent of dipping a toe in the water. With that mission being so successful, they should be ready to begin in earnest. The documents we've seen call for a massive strike into Empire territory with their entire fleet, hitting perhaps a dozen planets at once, leaving an occupation team behind, and moving on to more worlds in quick succession. In just a few days they could take a major bite out of the Empire, then dig in and prepare themselves for another major offensive. The documents were unclear in this regard, but it looks as though they mean to cut a path through from Omicron to the Caronamine Cluster, isolating nearly a third of our planets on the other side and making them easy targets to be picked off at leisure.'

'But will they go through with these plans now that we know about them?' the Empress persisted.

'Again we have to rely on what little we know about Gastaadi psychology,' von Wilmenhorst replied. 'They know that some of our people were on Omicron, broke into their headquarters, and then escaped again, but they can't be sure how much information they took with them. If I were in charge of their planning I'd have to make the assumption that all the plans were compromised and start from scratch – but it might not be that simple. For one thing, as Cesare can tell you, it's no easy task to bring your entire fleet together in one place for a major assault; the logistics are staggering, and once you've gone to so much trouble you might be reluctant to rethink your strategy. For another, there's the Gastaadi disdain for an opponent it beat so easily on Omicron. Even if we know their plans, the Gastaadi know it will take us time to build up our own forces to counter them, and they don't have much respect for us anyway. They could just bull ahead in spite of us, confident they can overcome anything we throw in their path.'

The Empress stared thoughtfully into space for a few moments, digesting the unhappy news her advisors had given her. The two men waited silently, unwilling to interrupt her train of thought. Finally she focused again and looked at them. '*Khorosho*, my lords, what is your recommendation?'

'We must prepare instantly for all-out war,' Admiral Benevenuto said without hesitation. 'A complete mobilization. It would take us a couple of weeks to get the entire fleet together from the outlying regions, but we could have nearly two-thirds assembled within four days. We would leave a sizeable guard around Earth itself, in case the Gastaadi mount a sneak attack, and there would be an emergency craft to evacuate you and any other high officials you designated if the situation became too dire. For the bulk of our fleet, we have two options – either we could wait and intercept the Gastaadi as they sweep in, or we could try a pre-emptive strike against the position we know they're holding at present.'

Edna Stanley looked to von Wilmenhorst, and the Head nodded his agreement with Benevenuto's plan.

The Empress was still hesitant. 'I must say, I don't like it. Aside from a few bloody rebellions the Empire's never been to war. I hate to be the one to set a precedent like this. We haven't even *tried* talking peace with the Gastaadi. Perhaps there's some way we could negotiate before we commit ourselves to fighting.'

Von Wilmenhorst shook his head sadly. 'None of us are very happy at the idea, and I understand perfectly how you feel . . .'

'Do you?' Edna snapped harshly. 'Do you know what it's like to make a decision that will commit trillions of citizens to a war against some unknown enemy – a war that could be the most devastating and brutal in human history?' Her voice softened again as she returned to her normally cool demeanor. 'You're good men, both of you, but you're so used to pushing ships and spies around on your gameboards I get the impression you sometimes lose track of the fact there are real people out there whose lives are at stake. The people *are* the Empire: I may hold the ultimate authority, but I'm also ultimately responsible to them. I never allow myself to forget that. The Stanley Dynasty has endured this long because we've held the citizens' trust; even the few really wretched monarchs have been tolerated for the sake of the good ones.

'Every time I make a decision or issue an edict, I wonder what the common citizens will think about it. Will it help them or hurt them; will it make the Empire a better place to live, or will it benefit only the elite few? Gentlemen, can I really commit *my* people to a horrible, bloody war without at least exploring some avenues for peace?'

The two men were silent for a moment; then von Wilmenhorst spoke up. 'Perhaps sometimes we are guilty of depersonalizing the conflicts we plan, but we still have the same ultimate objective: the welfare of the Empire. And in this particular case, I'm afraid negotiation will do us no good at all. Again, it's a matter of the Gastaadi psychology. As far as they're concerned, we're in an inferior position. We lost a planet and then we try to negotiate with them; to them it's a sign of desperation, of bargaining out of weakness. Their method of dealing with that is to mount more attacks. They simply won't bargain with someone they don't respect, and they won't respect us until we've shown them we can stand up and fight as well as they can. We didn't ask for this war, we didn't want it, but it's been shoved in our faces and we've got it whether we like it or not. If we wait, we encourage them to come in and ravage the Empire. If we fight now, perhaps we can impress them enough to talk peace. A short fight at the beginning might save millions of lives later on.'

The Empress looked at the two men, studying their faces carefully. 'You're both resolved on this, then?' When they nodded gravely, she took a deep sigh and continued. 'You're the two people I trust most on matters of imperial security. You've been proved right time and time again; I'd be a fool not to listen to you now despite my own misgivings. I'd rather not be remembered as the first empress to lead her people into war, but these dubious honors often come unbidden.

'Cesare, you said we had a choice of either sitting back and defending against their planned strike or else taking the battle to them. I choose the latter. If we're going to make them respect us, then by damn we're going to go all out. They've already breached our territory; we won't wait for them to come a millimeter further in. If we can

156

mount a decent strike force, I insist we take the initiative. If we hit them hard enough, they'll see we mean business and maybe they'll sit down and talk.'

'About mounting that strike force,' Benevenuto began slowly, but the Empress cut him off before he could finish.

'Yes,' she said, 'you mentioned their fleet is bigger than ours and you could only get two-thirds of ours together in time. Even with surprise on our side, that leaves us at a disadvantage, doesn't it?'

Von Wilmenhorst cleared his throat. 'There is the standing offer of an alliance.'

'So I recall.' Edna Stanley slumped ever so slightly in her chair: for the first time von Wilmenhorst could ever remember, she actually looked old. '*Bozhe moi*, how I hate the thought of dealing with that woman.'

'No more than I do,' the Head acknowledged, 'but she's delivered on her promise so far and we do need her help.'

'She's promised enough ships to bring our fleet up to complement if we make the attack,' Benevenuto added.

'But at what ultimate price?' the Empress muttered. '*Khorosho*, how do I get in touch with her?'

'I thought it best not to bring her here physically,' the Head said. 'With her robot body she'd be difficult to restrain and might pose a threat to you. She's still up at Luna Base: there's a direct access line open.' At the Empress's nod, the Head touched some controls on the side of the table and a triscreen hidden in the wall lit up to show Lady A's features.

The Empress's enemy had seldom looked more regal. She'd admitted to surreptitious ownership of an apartment in Moscoviense, the support town around Luna Base proper, and had gotten new clothes from there. She was currently wearing a malachite-colored bias-cut gown of panné velvet with a cloak of rare Falstaffi silver fur draped over her shoulders. Her hair was braided and coiled to resemble a crown, and her earrings were oval emerald pendants with small computer chips embedded in them. When she saw Edna watching her, she let the cloak slip off her shoulders to show a chip embroidered on her gown as an imperial crest.

'Hello, Edna,' she said casually. 'I trust the situation has been adequately explained to you.'

'You will show me the proper respect!' Edna stormed.

Lady A showed no fear at this display of imperial temper. 'You forget who you're talking to. I was the intimate of an emperor, your grandfather. As a matter of fact, we once made love on the floor under that very table you're seated at. But for the quirks of fate and genetics, child, I would be Empress and you my granddaughter.'

'Considering what happened to your real granddaughter, I'm very glad I'm not.'

'You can't hurt my feelings with old accusations, and time is short. Do you want my help against the Gastaadi?'

'What was your price?'

'As I told Zander before, I want governance of all worlds we take from the Gastaadi, to be independent of the Empire. You can keep your realm intact, and I get to build an empire of my own. It's a small price, giving away something that isn't yours in the first place.'

'I'm worried about deals that sound too good. Besides, my advisors tell me we don't really need you.'

'Either you're lying or they're bigger fools than I thought. If you say no, I'll simply take my organization underground. The Gastaadi will come slashing through the Empire. Perhaps they'll win, perhaps you will. But whoever wins will be weakened from the fight, while my troops will be nice and fresh. I'll pick apart the winner and take what I want. Remember, I've got time on my side. I took seventy years to build an organization to challenge you, I can wait another seventy if I have to.'

'All that presupposes I let you return to your organization,' Edna said.

'*Khorosho*. I'm a self-admitted traitor, and the punishment is death. I'm on Luna Base, surrounded by people with blasters who could carry out an execution order at any moment. If you don't need me, kill me now – because if you let me leave, it means the end of the Empire.'

The two women stared at one another through the triscreen, a duel of wills waged across nearly four hundred thousand kilometers that separated Earth and the Moon. Lady A was making a power play, naked and unashamed. She knew the cards she held, and she knew her adversary didn't dare execute her while this external threat to the Empire's security still existed. She appeared to relish throwing the challenge in her enemy's face.

For her part, Edna Stanley also knew the ground rules of this game. She'd let herself be suckered into playing it by rising to the other woman's bait of insolence. Now she either had to kill an ally she needed to save the Empire or else back down and lose face.

Brought up as she'd been on the values her father taught her, there was no question which choice she'd make. The safety of the Empire had to come before her own personal gratification. She cursed herself mentally for being foolish enough to be led down this path, and chalked it up as a lesson well learned. Yielding to Lady A on this point would be personally embarrassing, but it would never show in the history books; losing a war and millions of lives to a barbaric enemy would.

'As it turns out,' Edna said aloud, 'I've overruled my advisors and decided we do need your ships, after all. Your life is spared for the moment. I'll keep your confession in mind, though, for the proper occasion.

'As to your terms, I will agree to give you custody of all Gastaadi worlds we manage to take from them, if there are any. You and the Gastaadi probably deserve one another. The number of worlds you'll get will depend on any final peace settlement we make with the enemy . . .'

'Then I must be a party to all treaty negotiations,' Lady A interrupted. 'I won't have you dealing away my worlds haphazardly just so you can have some peace.'

'Agreed,' Edna said without hesitation. 'As for your ships, however, they will fight as part of the Imperial Navy. They will coordinate their efforts with my high command and they won't initiate any actions without Navy approval. Is that clear?'

'Perfectly,' Lady A nodded. As long as she was getting her way in the important things, she was willing to concede minor points. 'I can have my fleet assembled in three days, prepared for battle. I presume you'll want my ships to rendezvous with the Navy for concerted action.'

Von Wilmenhorst cleared his throat and entered the conversation for the first time. 'As I recall, milady, the last time some of our ships tried to rendezvous with some of yours, it was a trap and the area was mined.'

Unruffled, Lady A shrugged. '*Khorosho*, if you don't feel you can trust your ally in so vital a matter, you can pick the coordinates for the rendezvous. It makes little difference to me. I'd suggest, though, that you pick a site near the border of Gastaadi territory so we can take appropriate action as soon as our fleets are integrated.'

'We'll be in touch,' Admiral Benevenuto said. Lady A nodded and broke the connection. Her face vanished from the triscreen, but the force of her presence continued to be felt in the chamber.

'Let's finish this briefing as quickly as possible,' the Empress told her two advisors. 'I want to go take a long bath. Dealing with that woman makes me feel slimy all over.'

\* \* \*

Decisions were made, plans were drawn up, orders were given. The enormous and delicate machinery that was the Imperial Navy began to gear up for the first real war in its history. Heretofore the Navy had dealt only with pirates and rebels; now it would face the true test of meeting an outside force superior in some ways to itself.

Some of the Navy's ships were at the other end of the Empire, simply too far away to make a timely rendezvous before the attack against the Gastaadi must occur. Their task would be to spread themselves throughout the Empire, serving as guardians to the other worlds should the main fleet meet with catastrophe. They would probably not be able to defeat the Gastaadi forces *en masse*, but if the enemy were to invade deeper within the Empire its fleet would necessarily have to spread thinner and the Navy ships left behind would have more of a chance against the diluted armada.

Other ships were in dock for repairs. While some were only due for routine maintenance and were ordered to join the main fleet, some were totally out of commission. Repair crews were ordered to work around the clock to get those vessels in shape for future fighting.

They were not told why this was necessary: as far as they knew it was merely to prepare for an unscheduled series of war games. Edna did not want to alarm her people prematurely, since there was nothing as yet the common people could do but worry. The only people who would be told the true situation were the personnel aboard the ships that would do the actual fighting – and they would hear the news only after they'd reached the rendezvous point, when there was no chance of word leaking out and panicking the populace.

Captain Fortier requested a billet somewhere within the fighting fleet, and was granted a post on the flagship as part of Lord Admiral Benevenuto's evaluation team. He

161

had to leave in such a hurry that he had no chance to say goodbye to Helena in person; they had to settle for a hurried and awkward conversation over the communicator circuits.

At Helena's invitation, Yvette came down to Earth to spend several days with her friend. Helena took a well-earned vacation from her work at the Service and the two women spent much time in each other's company talking about many things. They compared their personal dealings with the notorious Lady A and Yvette related her adventures on Omicron, revealing the shame she'd felt at being controlled so thoroughly in the slave camp. Helena verified that the helplessness was similar to nitrobarb, which she herself had experienced on the planet Sanctuary.

The night before the battle was to begin, they sat out on the balcony of Helena's penthouse apartment, looking up at the darkened sky. Not many stars could be seen through the ambient light of metropolitan Miami, but the brighter ones glimmered peacefully, giving no indication of the fierce battle that was to come. The women looked for the spot where the fight would be, but it was currently in the daytime hemisphere. They would never have been able to see anything there anyway; light from that region would take centuries to reach the Earth. Still, they would have liked to look at the spot where the fate of the Galaxy might well be decided.

'I'm sorry about Jules,' Helena said, broaching a subject they'd both avoided until now. 'He was pretty special to me; I can only imagine how much he meant to you.'

'*Merci*. We spent all our lives together, growing up and working for the Circus. Even though we knew one or the other of us might get killed in action at any time, I still feel like I've lost half myself. I love Pias very much and it sounds odd to say this, but I don't think I'd miss him quite this much if he were taken from me. I've known him for only a few years: Jules has been there all my life.' Yvette took a thoughtful sip of the orange juice Helena had provided and stared up at the night sky.

'We might've been sisters now,' Helena said. 'I could have loved Jules very much, if he'd let me. That was a particularly gallant thing he did, discouraging me from the start. A lot of men might have strung me along for awhile till they'd gotten what they could. He was too honest for that.'

'Honesty was a big part of it,' Yvette admitted. 'There was also the fact, as he pointed out at the time, that the physiological differences between one-gee and three-gee natives make intermarriage hazardous at best – plus the fact that your father was our boss, which would have caused no end of problems. And anyway, he and Vonnie were engaged since their teens; it really was a love match there.

'He did tell me,' she added in confidential tones, 'that he regretted having to make the choice. He did find you very attractive and he liked you since our first meeting, up there on the Headquarters roof.' She looked sadly at Helena. 'It's a shame no other men you found worthwhile shared his good taste.'

'Now that you mention it, Paul Fortier did propose to me – but it was the night Lady A came to visit, and so many important things have been happening I didn't want to mention it to anyone.'

'I hope you said yes,' Yvette said.

'Of course. I'm no fool. Now that I look at it logically, I can see that Paul has a lot of the same traits as Jules – strong, good-looking, intelligent, dedicated, adventuresome. They even have the same physique, because Paul's family came from DesPlaines a couple generations back. Since he was raised on a one-gee world, though, that's no problem. Yes, Paul and Jules have a lot in common, including . . .'

She looked away and took another sip of her drink. Yvette waited quietly under the stars for Helena to finish her thought. 'Including the fact that Paul is off now risking his life against the Gastaadi,' Helena said, almost inaudibly. 'He could die out there in the battle tomorrow, and there's nothing you or I or anyone can do about it.'

She turned and looked straight into her friend's face. 'I don't want that to happen, Yvette. I don't want to lose another man I love. I don't want to be alone again.'

The two women held onto one another for solace long into the night under the calm, uncaring gaze of the stars.

# CHAPTER 13

## *Visit to a Very Small Planet*

When Jules left the alien scoutship to knock out the blaster emplacements, he knew he would not be returning to it. He'd been in enough dangerous situations to know the odds against him. He had to make four passes at four heavily armed units. With his skills, he could probably make one; with luck, a second. Three would take a miracle, and four – he didn't even want to think about it.

Even if he succeeded beyond his wildest expectations, he knew the ship wouldn't wait for him. If Yvette had been in charge she might have taken the gamble – but with Lady A flying the scoutship, there was no chance at all. She and he had been enemies too long, ever since they first locked eyes in Bloodstar Hall years ago. He'd been useful to her on this mission, but that use had come to an end. Now she would be just as happy to see him dead and out of her hair. The scoutship would take off the instant Lady A was familiar with the controls and Jules had knocked out the last blaster emplacement. He had no misconceptions about that, which was why he'd bowed to the inevitable and ordered them to go anyway.

Still, he had a job to do – and with typical d'Alembert determination he was going to see it through either to its end or to his own. Climbing back into the copterbus, he started the controls and the big machine took off on its hazardous mission.

The first emplacement was almost too easy. Steering, as he was, a labyrinthine path between the parked space-ships, he was able to approach the site from an unexpected direction. His carefully hurled grenade struck right

165

near the power unit of the heavy-duty blaster, creating a massive explosion that totally annihilated the big gun and its crew. The ensuing shock wave bounced the copterbus around on the violent air currents, and Jules had to pause momentarily to steady his craft before he could continue.

That pause gave the other heavy-duties a chance to get him in their sights, and Jules found himself having to dodge maniacally through a crossfire of energy beams, any one of which could spell destruction. The one advantage he had was that these weapons had been designed for shooting at spaceships, and a target as small as his copterbus was much harder to find. Still, he had to pilot his craft with the abandon of a lunatic as he continued along his course.

The intensity of the blasterfire only increased as he neared the emplacement on the east side of the landing field. Throwing the copter into a brief dive, he leaned out his hatch and tossed the second grenade. His aim wasn't quite as accurate as the first time, but it was close enough to achieve the desired results. With barely a backward glance at the havoc he'd wrought, Jules slued his craft around and headed for the southern emplacement.

He'd cut down his opposition now by a third, but the two remaining batteries fired on him with renewed determination. He was feeling lightheaded from his efforts, and knew it was an effect of all the adrenalin pumping through his body. He deliberately focused his attention on the blaster at the southern end, reminding himself sternly that it only took one hit to knock him out of the sky.

That hit came a bare instant later, as a beam from the southern emplacement sliced through the tail rotor of his copter. He fought the controls to try a quick adjustment, but the same beam continued through and nearly severed the entire rear of his vehicle. After that, everything was chaos. The copter was like a wild beast under his hands, bucking and rolling uncontrollably.

Jules knew he couldn't keep the copter in the air much longer, but he might have some choice in the matter of where it crashed. He'd knocked out two emplacements so far; if he could eliminate a third, the scoutship might still have a reasonable chance to escape successfully. He'd use the copter itself as a weapon against that third blaster site.

The southern emplacement was almost below him, still firing in his direction – but the unpredictability of the copter's motion made it as hard for the gunners to aim as it was for Jules to control. With almost nothing but sheer willpower, Jules directed his craft into a steep dive aimed precisely at the battery of blasters. This time he had the force of gravity on his side, pulling the copter downward at the proper angle to do maximum damage.

With his craft on a collision course, Jules unstrapped himself from the pilot's seat, opened the hatch beside him and leaped out into empty air with all the DesPlainian strength he could muster. Behind him, the copter-bus continued its suicidal plummet directly at the blasters, hitting them with an explosion that equaled those of the first and second emplacements together. An enormous ball of orange flame rose into the sky, followed moments later by a column of thick black smoke.

Jules himself had no time to appreciate the aesthetics of his actions. He was falling freely through the air with the ground rising to meet him. His body shared the downward speed of the copter at the time he'd leaped from it, modified slightly by the vector of his jump. All his thoughts were directed toward a safe landing and avoiding instant death on impact.

To a person from a three-gee planet, objects on a one-gee world seemed to fall in slow motion, just as objects on the Moon seemed to fall slower to someone accustomed to Earth's gravity. A fall from a great enough height could still be fatal, though. Jules had to use his quicker reflexes and his acrobatic skills to avoid such a fate.

As he approached the hard ground he tucked his knees up under his chin, forming himself into a compact ball. He was all prepared to hit the ground and roll, absorbing the momentum of his fall the way he and Yvette had done so many times at the climax of their circus act. He might have made a perfect landing, but for the fact that the fireball from the copter's crash rose into the sky just as he was about to land. The concussion of the blast knocked him slightly sideways along his intended path, and even with his reflexes there was no time to readjust.

He landed and rolled as he intended, but a sharp stab of pain seared through the left side of his body. He cried out in agony and flopped over on his side, lying still on the damp ground. His left leg was throbbing with waves of pain that made thinking impossible. For several minutes he lay helpless on the grass, gasping for breath and trying hard to fight his way through the pain back to clear thought again.

A dull roar sounded far off and Jules opened his eyes, squinting against the bright artificial lights the aliens had turned on. From this angle the world looked upside-down and strange, and not a little blurry, but he could make out the shape of the scoutship taking off into the sky. The one remaining blaster emplacement was firing at the ship with all its power, but that wasn't enough to penetrate the scoutship's sturdy shields. Within seconds the vessel had zoomed safely out of sight into the upper atmosphere and the reaches of space beyond.

Jules closed his eyes again as more waves of pain washed over him. He'd done as much as he could to ensure the success of the mission. If he were to die now, it would be with the knowledge that Earth had been warned about the alien menace. In fact, as he lay on the ground in pain, he almost wished some of the aliens would come along to find him and put him out of his misery. At least it would stop the pain in his leg.

But several minutes passed and no aliens came, and Jules's instincts for survival reasserted themselves. He was alive, albeit with one injured leg, and life to a d'Alembert meant action. If he could get away from this area, there was a chance he could make it to one of the cities and join up with a band of the freedom fighters, as he'd told Yvette he'd do. His duty to Earth wasn't over yet, not as long as there was a chance he could help liberate Omicron from its oppressors. There was still work for him to do.

But he couldn't do it lying here. The aliens probably thought he'd been killed in the copter crash, and they were preoccupied with putting out the fires his attacks had caused, but that state of affairs wouldn't last forever. He couldn't just lie here on the ground and expect not to be seen. Bad leg or not, he had to reach some safe place to hide before he was discovered.

Rolling over onto his right side he propped himself up on his elbow and gingerly felt down along his left leg. He hadn't heard anything snap when he landed and the pain, though agonizing, felt more like a sprain than a break. He made the tentative diagnosis of a sprained knee. He wished he had something to wrap it with to prevent swelling, but the only material on hand was the jumpsuit he was wearing, and it was too tough to tear into strips. He would have to let the sprain heal along its own course, even though he knew the throbbing pain would be tremendous.

Looking around, he assessed the situation in terms of hiding places. To the north of him was the aliens' landing field with its forest of spaceships standing silent and ominous. To the south was the road to the now-defunct slave camp. To the west, still burning, was the battery of blasters his copter had just destroyed, and beyond that the banks of the Long River. To the east lay the headquarters building he'd so recently assaulted, and beyond that, a thousand meters away, were the hills that led into natural forest.

All directions were difficult, but Jules decided on the east as his best bet. If he could reach those forested hills, he might find some hiding place from alien searches until his leg was well-enough healed for serious traveling.

Slowly and carefully he pulled himself up into a crouch balanced on his good right leg. After checking the area to make sure no aliens could spot him, he straightened up and began hopping in his chosen direction. Each hop brought with it a new stab of pain as the jarring motion disturbed the already inflamed tissue around his left knee. In addition, hopping across the uneven ground was a strain on his good leg because, without any objects around to lean against, the right leg had to maintain the precarious balance. Jules found he had to stop every few meters to crouch again and catch his breath. This was going to be a rougher journey than he'd thought.

He'd made it almost as far as the headquarters building when he saw a platoon of alien soldiers walking through the woods in the hills where he was heading. Perhaps they were looking for more saboteurs, or perhaps it was a routine patrol of some sort. Whatever it was, it meant he'd have to change his plans for hiding out, and quickly: he was out in the open here, and likely to be spotted at any moment.

Near the headquarters was the smaller shed that looked as though it might have been used for storage. It was the nearest place offering any refuge, and Jules took it. A couple of quick hops brought him to the door, which was unlocked. Pulling his blaster in case any aliens were inside, he threw the door open and lurched in. The shed was deserted, and Jules closed the door behind him again.

The shed was piled with large crates of miscellaneous construction materials. Jules hobbled among them, peering in the crates, and found one that was filled with some of the mylar-type fabric that the buildings were made of. With difficulty he pulled himself up over the edge of the crate and lowered himself into the mass of material. Burrowing in, he covered himself with a couple of layers so he wouldn't be seen by any aliens casually inspecting the crate. He had his blaster tucked into his lap in case any of the soldiers became more than casually interested.

He'd intended only to stay here for an hour or so, to let the throbbing in his leg subside a little and let the aliens around the building go about their business. But the shock from the injury to his leg finally caught up with him. That, coupled with all his exertion and the lack of sleep in the past night, brought unconsciousness almost as soon as he was sure he was safe from detection. Jules d'Alembert succumbed to a well-deserved sleep.

He was awakened by a jostling motion of the crate that caused his knee to bump the wall, sending a stab of pain through his body. He made a sharp gasp, but the sound was fortunately muffled by the building material around him. With his mind clouded by pain and the last vestiges of sleep, it took him a few moments to remember where he was. Then, as awareness came back to him, he gripped his blaster tighter and tried to figure out what was happening.

From the movement around him, he could tell his crate was being carried out of the shed. The most obvious thing that occurred to him was that the mylar-like material in the box was going to be used, possibly to repair the damage he'd done last night to the headquarters building.

If so, he'd have a fight on his hands when they opened the crate and found him inside. With his bad knee and the fact that he was fighting alone against so many, it would be a miracle if he survived. He braced himself once more for death.

But his box was not opened. After being carried for a while, it was set down for a few minutes. Jules debated getting out now, but there were too many sounds around indicating a lot of traffic in the area; he would be spotted for sure. For the moment it would be best if he stayed where he was.

Then the crate was lifted somewhere, carried on a level for a while, then taken down again. Extending all his senses as best he could, Jules heard clanking sounds and hollow echoes as though he were surrounded by metal walls. The air had a slight smell of machine oil. At a guess, he supposed his crate may have been loaded back onto one of the alien ships. Even if he wanted to get out and confirm his suspicions, he couldn't; another crate was stacked on top of his, and he didn't have the strength or the leverage to budge it. For the moment, he was trapped here.

His hunch was verified about an hour later, though, when he felt a familiar vibration that told him a spaceship was about to take off. He braced himself against the fabric as best he could; the acceleration came on and pressed him deeper into the material. It was a heavier acceleration than was normally used on human ships, straining even his DesPlainian limits. These aliens must be tougher than they looked if they could routinely withstand such accelerations. Of course, there was a chance this was a completely automated ship, in which case no concessions would need to be made to a flesh-and-blood crew. There was still air in the cargo hold for him to breathe, although that might be only a residual of what was left when the

172

ship was closed up on Omicron. Jules decided he'd better play it on the safe side and not exert himself, conserving as much oxygen as he could in case it wasn't replenished. In his condition, he didn't want to exert himself too much, anyway.

When sufficient time had elapsed after takeoff, Jules experienced the familiar feeling of the ship slipping into subspace. They were going on a long journey, whatever their goal; Jules wondered whether he'd become the first human to visit one of the aliens' worlds – and whether he'd welcome such a singular honor. Whatever happened, though, he hoped the trip would not take too long. He was getting very hungry, he was cramped, and he was in considerable pain from his throbbing leg. If the aliens were going home, he hoped they didn't live too far away.

After thirteen hours, the ship dropped back into normal space again. Jules's mind, ever alert to details, could calculate about how far they must have traveled, although he had no idea what their direction had been. That gave him a sphere with a very large radius, and he might be at any point on its surface.

Again there was a heavy pressure as the ship decelerated and came in for a landing. There was the hard bump of touchdown, and things became very quiet on the ship again. The first thing Jules noticed was the gravity – or rather, the lack of it. After such heavy deceleration, of course, even one gee would seem trivial by comparison, but this was lighter even than that. Wherever they'd landed, it was someplace small – a moon, perhaps, or an orbiting station of some kind.

Since he was still trapped by the crate on top of his, Jules could only wait. Eventually there were noises around him and the crate was taken off the top of his. Then his own crate was moved out of the ship and into a storage area of some kind. There were the sounds of activity around him for a while, then silence. The unloading had been completed and the storeroom sounded deserted. Jules decided to risk emerging from his hiding place to see where he was.

His body was cramped and stiff from its long confinement in a small space, and his knee was still sore, although the throbbing had stopped and the pain didn't make itself known unless he moved the knee. Jules pushed the fabric away from him and lifted himself to the top of the crate to look out on his new surroundings.

The room was pitch black, confirming Jules's hunch that he was in a storage area of some sort. He reached into a utility compartment of his belt and took out a pocketflash, which he shined around to get a better impression. Boxes and crates were scattered about the floor in orderly rows. There was enough gravity to hold things in place; now that he'd had a while to get used to it, he could estimate it at perhaps a tenth of a gee. On behalf of his injured leg, he was very grateful; light gravity meant less pressure he'd have to put on it while hobbling about.

With no aliens in sight, he climbed out of his crate and stood up again for the first time in almost two days. He had to lean against the side of the crate to take the weight off his left leg, but even so it felt good to be able to stretch again. Now if only he could find something to eat he'd feel almost human.

Using his pocketflash to guide him Jules limped painfully down the aisles of boxes until he came to a wall of the room, then followed that around until he found a door. He was surprised to see a palmplate beside it; it seemed odd that the aliens would use the same mechanisms for opening doors that humans did. Putting his ear to the door he listened for sounds from outside, but could detect nothing. Holding his blaster ready, he palmed the plate to open the door of the storeroom.

The door slid silently open to reveal a well-lit hallway beyond. Jules blinked at the sudden light, knowing that for a few moments, until his eyes could adjust to the brightness, he'd be an easy target. But the corridor was deserted and no one saw him standing there in the doorway. His luck was holding.

The hallway extended to the left and right as far as he could see. There was a slight curvature to it, reinforcing his guess that he might be on a space station whose gravity was generated artificially with ultragrav. There were doorways at intervals set into the walls, but no one else was in sight. He couldn't just stand here, so Jules started off to his left. The direction of his walk was not entirely random; this way he had the nearside wall to lean against as he moved, taking more pressure off his bad knee.

At each door he came to he listened, but could hear no sounds inside. He palmed the plates beside them and found more storerooms like the one he'd just left. This area, then, must be reserved for supplies and largely empty – a break for him, since he wasn't up to a fullscale battle right now. If his leg had been feeling better he might have examined the contents of the storerooms more carefully – but, injured as he was, he didn't have the energy for side excursions.

He'd just left one of the storerooms when he heard some noises coming his way. He ducked back inside the door and left it slightly ajar to see what happened outside.

As the noise came closer, he could discern it was the sound of voices – human voices. They were speaking Empirese in a normal conversational tone, as though unafraid of being detected by enemy aliens. Jules watched as they went by, and could see that the pair were a man and a woman dressed in coveralls and walking casually, as though being on an alien planet were a normal part of their existence.

The pair were talking about lunch as they walked past Jules's hiding place, a topic that only served to remind him he hadn't eaten in three days. But if his stomach was growling about its empty condition, his mind had plenty of food for thought.

Was he wrong in all his assumptions? Had he somehow ended up on a world within the Empire, rather than one of the aliens' planets? But how could that be? His crate had definitely been loaded on a spaceship near where it had been stored, and there were no human ships around, just alien vessels. It had to have been an alien ship that brought him here, and no such ship could have landed at any civilized port without attracting attention.

That left a possibility he didn't like at all. Could it be that some humans had sold out to the enemy, betraying their own race to these coldhearted killers? The thought made him burn with anger, yet a coldly analytical part of his mind was telling him it made some sense. That could explain how the aliens had gotten such good reconnaissance information about Omicron without anyone's noticing them, and how they seemed to know so much about conditions on human worlds while the Empire knew nothing about them. That would also explain why two humans dressed in coveralls could walk so casually through alien territory, talking without any worry of being overheard.

He had to investigate this matter at once: it could make an enormous difference in the way the Empire reacted to the alien threat. He waited for the pair to get far enough ahead of him, then he cautiously moved out of the storeroom and began following after them. He stayed close to the wall, as much to avoid being seen as to balance himself. This new mystery so intrigued him he almost forgot about his injured leg. Only an occasional stab of pain reminded him to take it easy.

He hardly needed to worry about being spotted; the people he was trailing were so secure they gave not a thought to the possibility of someone behind them. Even walking casually, though, they were able to move much faster than the limping Jules, and he dared not run to catch up. Their voices faded down the end of the corridor and they vanished from view completely.

Jules continued on in that direction anyway, and his patience soon was rewarded when he came to the doors that unmistakably marked an elevator tube, the kind used throughout the Empire. Beside the door was a sign written in plain Empirese:

> Storage: Level 38–41
> Materials Processing: Level 36–38
> Cafeteria: Level 35
> Manufacturing: Level 33

Just beyond the elevator tube, the corridor ended and became a balcony with a waist-high railing. Jules hopped over and leaned on the railing, looking down on the sight below him, and received the shock of his life.

Spread before him, five stories down, was a vast manufacturing complex laid out in an efficient assembly line. The line was idled now, and about half the lights had been turned off to save energy – but even in the dim lighting that remained, Jules could see some of the parts that were assembled on the line. Heads, torsos, and limbs of the green alien bodies were scattered about, waiting to be pieced together.

Jules realized now why the aliens didn't bleed. They were not living beings at all. They were merely machines, robots, built on this assembly line by human beings to serve human purposes. And that was the most frightening concept of all.

# CHAPTER 14

## *The Artificial Crisis*

The magnitude of this deception almost overwhelmed Jules. *Someone* had gone to the trouble of manufacturing thousands of the alien robots, along with their weapons, their ships, their equipment, and everything else connected with them. *Someone* had made up an entire language and culture for these artificial creatures. What was worse, *someone* had bombarded Omicron, killing millions of innocent people and forcing even more millions into a life of fear and bloodshed.

That someone had gone to enormous trouble and expense to pull off the most dastardly hoax in human history. Jules had more than a faint suspicion who that someone had to be, but as yet there was no certain proof. Even more puzzling than the *who*, though, was the *why* behind it all. It would be foolish to go to these lengths for no reason at all, and the people behind this were anything but foolish. But try as he would, Jules could not see what the expected gain was. Perhaps it was the hunger and the pain in his leg slowing down his normally brilliant mind, but he could see no sane reason for perpetrating these crimes. Of course, sanity wasn't a prerequisite, but some amount of logic should be there nonetheless – even if it was a twisted, criminal brand of reasoning.

One thing he knew for certain: it was vitally important for him to find out as much of the truth as he could behind the hoax and report it to the Empire as quickly as possible. He cursed the injury to his leg; now, more than ever before, he needed to be in top physical condition and the bad knee would hamper his movements terribly. Still, there was nothing to be done except make the best of it and get along somehow.

He spent the next few hours sneaking around the corridors, observing conditions on this enemy base. One thing in his favor was that uniforms did not seem to be worn here; the closest to a universal garment was the tailored gray-green coveralls worn by many of the workers. Uniforms, after all, were meant to separate one class of people from the general populace around them. If everyone here were part of the conspiracy, there would be no special outfit needed to set them apart.

After some searching, Jules found a laundry room and, when no one was looking, stole an approximately fitting pair of the coveralls. He stashed his jumpsuit, which was starting to smell bad, in one of the seldom-used storerooms, keeping his utility belt worn under the coveralls and his blaster and knives tucked discreetly away. Thus accoutered, he no longer had to slink stealthily through the corridors when no one else was around; he could walk boldly down the halls, looking as though he was on his way somewhere important, without fear of being spotted.

There were some difficulties, of course. Everyone on this base had an ID card. The cards allowed access to certain rooms which were off limits to the general personnel, and kept credit tabs for everyone so they could charge meals at the cafeterias. Jules couldn't very well steal one, because its theft would be quickly reported and his movements could be traced through the use of that card. To be a totally invisible person on this base, he had to be invisible to its computer as well.

One of his first acts after donning his new clothes was to find the kitchens. These areas were not secured, and Jules was able to wander through them at will, pretending to be a new helper assigned to aid the cooks, and sampling food in the meantime. At long last he was able to relieve the oppressive hunger that had dogged him since before leaving Omicron, and that in turn enabled him to think and act more clearly.

Stationed at intervals throughout the maze of corridors were directories showing where most of the important sections of the base were. Jules quickly memorized the directions, and over the next week treated himself to a complete tour of the facility.

His initial impression of this place was correct. It was a planetoid some twenty kilometers in diameter that had been hollowed out and reconstructed as a space base. The interior was honeycombed with levels, corridors, manufacturing facilities, living quarters, even recreational facilities for the people who spent their lives working for whoever had established this base. It was a world in miniature dedicated to the manufacture of items that would be used to subvert the Empire.

The more Jules saw, the more impressed – and worried – he became. This base did not just manufacture robots that looked like aliens, but a variety of other things as well. There was one separate section that manufactured weapons and armaments; Jules had helped destroy one such illegal plant on the planet Slag several years ago, and this one seemed to have taken up the slack with almost no trouble at all. And fully half of the base seemed geared to producing spacecraft parts. Jules was even able to don a spacesuit and go out on the surface of the planetoid, where there were vast and largely automated shipyards for the construction of spaceships.

Most ominous of all, the Directory referred to this place as 'Spacebase 4.' The inherent assumption was that there were at least three other bases like this established elsewhere in space, also turning out ships, weapons, and who knew how many other devices for the overthrow of the Empire of Earth.

Jules couldn't go to the normal worker dormitories to sleep for fear of being discovered in the wrong bed. He ended up spending a lot of his time in the storerooms, both sleeping and resting. Even the one-tenth gee was enough to cause discomfort to his sore knee, and he had to retire frequently to a private place so he could rest up from his exertions.

The rests gave him a much-needed chance to think over all he'd seen, but still there were no clearcut answers to who or why. The scale of this operation was simply enormous, easily involving millions of rubles and thousands of workers. There couldn't be many organizations capable of functioning on that kind of a level; whatever this was, Jules knew he was close to the heart of a syndicate with galaxywide connections and ambitions.

After roaming through the base for a full week, Jules had seen pretty much all there was to be seen, and had gathered all the information about the base's workings that could be gleaned from simple observations. And still the motivation behind the hoax eluded him. He was left with two choices. He could either escape back to Earth right now aboard one of the supply ships that regularly stopped at the base, and tell the Head everything he'd seen – or he could try some direct action and take a bit of a risk in order to learn more about the mysterious motivation.

The information he had right now was valuable enough; being previously unsuspected, it would give the Head plenty to think about. But Jules hated to leave a job only partially done. There was more information yet to be obtained, and unless he got that as well his mission here would not be a complete success.

There was a man named Dom Ferrera who seemed to

be the boss of the entire station. His name was signed prominently at the bottom of various memoranda that were posted in public places around the base, and he was listed as having a suite of offices in the control level near the center of the planetoid. If anyone around this place had the answers Jules needed, it would be Ferrera. Jules decided it would be worth the additional risk to capture this Gospodin Ferrera and ask him a few questions.

He set about stalking his quarry with the famous d'Alembert determination. Ferrera stayed almost entirely on the inner levels of the base, where Jules's lack of an identity card prevented him from going into many of the rooms. Still, after hours of careful surveillance, his patience was rewarded: Dom Ferrera came walking alone down the corridor toward Jules. He barely even noticed Jules was there, so preoccupied was he with some matter that was on his mind. Jules waited until the man had gone past him, then followed him until they reached a deserted section of the hall.

Suddenly Jules was at Ferrera's side, the muzzle of his blaster digging into Ferrera's ribs. 'If you want to live, *tovarishch*, you'll come quietly with me,' Jules said.

Ferrera was not a man to argue with a blaster, and accompanied Jules up a nearby elevator tube to one of the disused storerooms. Once inside, Jules pushed the man brusquely so he fell into a corner by some crates. 'What is this?' Ferrera asked angrily, trying to salvage some of his dignity.

'You might say it's an inquisition,' Jules replied. 'I've got some questions for you and I want answers. As it happens, I don't have any nitrobarb or detrazine with me, so I'll just have to rely on the old fashioned method of extracting information – pain. As long as you keep giving me answers I can believe, you'll be fine. But I have little sympathy for anyone who'd manufacture alien monsters

182

and kill several million people, so lies and silences will be punished accordingly. Are you in charge of this base?'

Ferrera nodded glumly.

'Who's your boss?' Jules asked.

'I don't know.'

Jules fired his blaster into the side of a crate, just a couple of centimeters from Ferrera's ear. 'I don't believe someone as important as you wouldn't know who he reports to.'

'I . . . I don't know their names, that's what I meant. There's a woman, very beautiful, but I only know her as Lady A. And there's someone they call C, but I've never seen him; I just get his orders over the teletype.'

A cold fire raged in Jules's heart and mind. His worst suspicions had proved correct; Lady A was behind this whole scheme, meaning she was directly responsible for all those deaths on Omicron. His hatred of her, which he'd thought was absolute before, reached new depths as he realized what a calculating, coldblooded murderess she really was. No wonder, even as a young woman, she'd earned the epithet 'The Beast of Durward.' To Jules that seemed too kind a description; few beasts he'd ever heard of were capable of such wanton savagery.

He kept his rage well-buried, though, in front of Ferrera. He still had an interrogation to conduct, and he had to keep it as professional as possible. Ferrera, a natural coward, kept answering satisfactorily to the best of his knowledge. Slowly but surely, under Jule's deft guidance, a picture of the true situation began to emerge.

The first of the spacebases were started up about seven years ago. There were now nine of them as far as Ferrera knew, all located beyond the boundaries of the Empire so the Navy was unlikely to stumble across them. At first they were solely for the construction of the conspiracy's fleet of spaceships, but a few years ago they started manufacturing weapons and munitions as well. Then, just a little over a year ago, they tooled up to manufacture the alien robots in mass quantities, as well as alien-looking weapons and ships.

Ferrera insisted he didn't know the full reason behind the alien hoax; Lady A never trusted her subordinates enough to give any of them more information than they needed to operate. But from talking with some of the conspiracy's ship's officers, he'd gotten the impression she wanted to lure the imperial fleet into a crossfire between her own ships and the supposed aliens, which were also hers.

As Jules listened, the plan suddenly became clearer in his mind. Two years ago, at Edna's coronation, the conspiracy had made a direct assault on Earth. They'd been rebuffed after a major battle, and ended up losing nearly two-thirds of their fleet. Even though, according to Ferrera, they'd been engaged in a feverish rebuilding plan since then, they still did not have enough ships to try such a direct assault again. Instead, they were returning to their old tactics of misdirection and treachery to win the day for them.

Lady A was willing to sacrifice a planet in order to win an empire, and the planet she chose was Omicron. She wanted to convince the Empire there was a threat to its security so serious that it would consider an alliance with her as its only alternative. To the end she spared no expense to make the danger look real, and she made sure the Empire's most reliable agents would be along with her to investigate and confirm the findings. At the same time, she accompanied them so they didn't stray too far behind the scenes and see the props that held up the scenery. Jules had almost done so when he noticed the aliens didn't bleed; Lady A had negated that finding, not by denying it, but by agreeing it was interesting and then, logically, directing his attention elsewhere.

The point of this charade was to allow her own ships to be integrated into the imperial fleet. The combined armada would then go off and confront the enemy. At a crucial moment in the battle Lady A's ships would suddenly betray their supposed allies, catching the Navy in a deadly crossfire between the 'aliens' and the conspiracy's forces. The treachery would be so unexpected it would demoralize the Navy, and few of the ships caught in the trap could be expected to survive. After that, the rest of the Empire would be easy targets for the conspiracy to pick off at its leisure.

'When is this battle supposed to take place?' Jules asked coldly, working hard to keep the fury out of his voice.

'I don't know, exactly. It could be any time now. The ships left a couple of days ago to take their various positions.'

Jules felt a chill. He might already be too late. 'Where is the battle going to take place?'

'That depends on the Empire's strategists. If they go after the alien fleet, it will be at a position we've told them the aliens are rendezvousing. If not, they might wait for the alien fleet to come to them.'

If they were going to attack the alien fleet, they would do it quickly, Jules reasoned. Therefore, he ought to try that point first. If there was nothing there, he could send a subcom message to Earth, warning them.

'Where's the rendezvous spot?' he asked Ferrera.

'I don't have the coordinates memorized,' the base's leader said. 'They're somewhere in my office. I can get them for you . . .'

'We'll get them together, comrade,' Jules said. 'I'll be right at your side every step of the way. At the slightest hint of trouble you'll be past caring how it turns out; I'm very good with this.' He waved the blaster to emphasize his point.

185

They left the storeroom and returned to the administration level. Jules kept his blaster discreetly out of sight, but left no doubt in Ferrera's mind that it was pointed at him. The administrator gave Jules no trouble along the way, and used his ID card to get them through the back door into his private office.

Ferrera walked over to his computer terminal. 'It'll take a second to retrieve the information you need,' he said as his hands went to the keyboard.

Jules pressed the muzzle of his blaster up against the back of Ferrera's neck. 'If you press one wrong key, it'll be the last one,' he promised.

Working slowly and nervously, explaining what he was doing at each step, Ferrera typed in his ID number and requested the rendezvous coordinates from the base's central computer. As the coordinates appeared on the screen, Jules memorized them and made a rough mental calculation of where they might translate to in real terms.

The mental calculation broke his concentration for just a second, and Ferrera must have sensed that. Giving Jules a quick kick to the left leg, where he'd seen him limping, the station's boss pushed the SOTE agent away and reached for a drawer of his desk where he kept a gun of his own. Jules cried out in pain and fell backwards, but fired even as he was falling.

The beam caught Ferrera in the small of his back before he could even get his weapon out of the desk drawer. He fell forward onto the desk, but one of his last acts before dying was to press the alarm button to indicate trouble. Sirens and alarms started sounding throughout the administrative level.

Jules picked himself painfully off the ground, favoring his left leg. He knew he was in no condition to fight an entire station's worth of security guards, just as he knew he had to escape quickly to let the Empire know about the treachery it was facing. Lacking the needed muscle, he would have to count on finesse to get himself out of here.

Reaching into his coveralls, he took out one of the remaining grenades Yvette had given him. He went to the door of the office, tossed the grenade toward the back of the room, and leaped through the doorway just as it went off. The explosion shook the entire floor and demolished the room beyond all recognition.

People, including the security guards with guns drawn, were racing to the scene from all directions. 'Over here, help!' Jules called to them. 'There's a saboteur, a spy. He blew up Ferrera's office, now he's getting away.'

'What happened?' one of the guards said, helping Jules to his feet in the corridor outside the office.

'I was in there talking about production schedules when a man came in. He shot Ferrera, threw in a bomb, then ran away. I was lucky to get out of there. Ow, I hurt my leg, too.'

'Who was it?' another guard asked.

'Don't know, never saw him before. Tall guy with red hair and a beard. He ran down toward C-station elevator tube. That's all I saw.'

The guards raced off in the indicated direction, radioing the description of the imaginary culprit to their comrades and blocking off all escape routes to that side of the base. Jules stood around with the other office workers for a while, answering questions about the attack and accepting their congratulations for still being alive. Finally he excused himself on the grounds he had to visit the infirmary to take care of his leg. He elicited nothing but sympathy as he limped down the corridor and out of everyone's view.

He proceeded as quickly as he could to the supply loading station where several ships were currently docked, off-loading supplies for the base. Word of the disturbance had spread here by this time, but none of the details was very clear. Jules took full advantage of the confusion.

'I'm with security,' he identified himself to the ship's captain. Before the skipper could ask for proof, Jules continued, 'You may have heard we just had an incident of sabotage down in administration. We think the saboteur came aboard in one of the recent ships, possibly yours. There may be more hiding somewhere. Get all your crew out on deck, immediately.'

When the captain started to protest this highhanded treatment, Jules drew his blaster. 'I have no time to argue, Captain. We're dealing with saboteurs who are desperate and will stop at nothing. You wouldn't want it put in your report that you helped them get away, would you?'

When put that way, the captain had no choice but to comply. He ordered his crew to line up outside the ship on the double. As the crew fell in, Jules walked up and down their ranks, examining each one carefully. 'This is all your people, Captain?' he asked.

'Yes, and I'll vouch for every single one of them,' the skipper said.

Jules nodded. '*Khorosho*, but the saboteur could still be hiding somewhere in the ship. I'm going in to search. There'll be more of my people along in a minute; send them in after me, but keep your own crew here. We wouldn't want any of them shot by mistake, would we?'

As the captain agreed to keep his crew out of Jules's way, the SOTE agent entered the ship and went straight for the control room. The ship was fueled and everything seemed in order, so Jules closed the outer hatch by remote control. At this point the captain realized something was amiss, but it was far too late. Within minutes, Jules had detached the ship from its mooring at the base and pulled away into the darkness of space.

The base was not a military complex, and there were no ships available to chase after him. Jules accelerated rapidly to the needed speed for the switch to subspace, and made the drop unhindered. But there was little time to congratulate himself on his escape. He grimly set in the coordinates of the alien rendezvous spot, hoping with all his might he wouldn't arrive there to find the shattered hulks of the Empire's fleet already awaiting him.

# CHAPTER 15

## *The Gastaadi War*

Quickly the forces of the Empire gathered. They came from Luna Base and from all the Sectors of the Galaxy to fight against the first enemy mankind had ever encountered. They did not know why they were summoned, at first, but they were loyal to their orders. Small gunboats, scoutships, cruisers, destroyers, battleships, all the way up to the superdreadnoughts – all took their places in the grand formation that was the one real hope of saving the Empire from the Gastaadi menace.

Never before in history had such a large percentage of the Imperial fleet been assembled in one place for a common purpose. The very act of coordinating all these vessels required a cadre of senior officers. When battle came, these various units would have to fight as a unified whole. If anyone got in the way of anyone else, the entire venture could quickly devolve into a rout, and the Empire itself might be lost.

Lord Admiral Benevenuto, aboard the flagship *Valiant*, watched the entire mission come together on the enormous three-dimensional display screen in the central viewing hall. He was inundated by reports from his aides, relaying messages that this squadron was short on fuel or that cruiser had malfunctioning gunsights, and he had to take all these myriad factors into account in organizing the entire fleet. Still, every so often he took a few seconds away from the minutiae to observe the progress in the big display screen, and could not help but be impressed with what he saw. A maneuver this large and complex should have taken weeks to arrange; instead, they were managing it in a matter of days. In spite of the small mishaps which were an offshoot of any milit ry maneuver, he felt justifiably proud of the Navy he'd spent his life serving.

The outcomes of battles were always a gamble. Earth might not defeat the Gastaadi forces, but the Empire would always know its men and women had done their best for freedom in the Galaxy.

Just as the imperial fleet was pulling into shape, the ships of Lady A's conspiracy arrived right on schedule for their rendezvous. Benevenuto frowned at the thought of having to admit a force of unknown capability and unknown trustworthiness into his ranks, but he knew the additional numbers would be needed if they were to stand a chance against the Gastaadi menace. The conspiracy's forces would make up roughly one-quarter of the total fleet, and more time was spent assigning them places and integrating them into the chain of command.

After the hours and days of preparing, everything was at last in readiness for the attack on the Gastaadi fleet. Before leaving their own location, Benevenuto opened a channel to all ships in his flotilla, Lady A's as well as the Navy's. For the first time, the ordinary crewpeople were informed of the true nature of their mission. Benevenuto spoke in blunt terms about the enemy's method of capturing and subduing the planet Omicron, and told them how vulnerable the Empire would be to attack from outside if this mission were a failure. He emphasized the death and destruction that might rain down on their individual home planets, killing their loved ones, if the Gastaadi were victorious. And finally, he told them that, if all patriots held together, he knew they would defeat the enemy and push them back into their own portion of the Galaxy where they belonged.

It was a moving and masterful speech. In all the Navy's ships there was not a heart left unstirred nor a soul that was not determined to fight at top form against the alien marauders who, for no apparent reason, threatened the peace and security of an Empire that had done them no wrong.

Lord Admiral Benevenuto was pleased with what he'd done. As the ships reported back their readiness for combat, he gave the order for the fleet to accelerate forward. When all ships were up to speed, the flotilla made the drop into subspace *en masse*, a precision maneuver unparalleled in military history.

There followed a nervous several hours as the Earth fleet proceeded to the coordinates where the Gastaadi forces were assumed to be massing. Benevenuto was plagued with doubts. What if commands got fouled up and the flotilla did not all appear back in regular space simultaneously? There had never been an invasion of this magnitude before, and there were innumerable things that could go wrong. What if commands between the Navy and Lady A's ships fell apart, causing friction between the allies? Would the lack of coordination cause a serious problem to their common effort?

His worst fear, though, was that they'd reach the designated spot and find nothing there; that the enemy, realizing its security had been breached, had dispersed its ships again – or worse, had decided to launch its own attack into the Empire while the Navy was involved in an elaborate and expensive attack on empty space. Although Benevenuto had retired to his private cabin to rest before the upcoming battle, he found no rest forthcoming. His mind was too far filled with the possible horrors that could occur.

He was on the bridge, though, mind alert, when the flotilla returned to normal space at precisely the spot they'd been aiming for. There on the screen was the mass of glowing dots representing the Gastaadi fleet, not too far distant from their own as had been predicted. The enemy force was smaller than they'd been led to expect, perhaps only two-thirds the size of their own fleet, but Benevenuto was not going to question such good luck. Maybe some of the enemy ships had been dispersed, but the bulk of them were here and it was still a sizeable force to deal with. Since his ships now outnumbered the enemy, he contemplated an easier time delivering a crippling blow to the Gastaadi plans for conquest.

As soon as all reports came in assuring him his formation was intact, Benevenuto gave the order to move forward and join in battle with the enemy. With deliberate speed the ships of the Empire closed the gap between themselves and the Gastaadi. The alien fleet remained motionless in space, holding its position bravely against the advancing foe. Within minutes the battle would commence.

Then, out of nowhere, a small ship came darting into the no-man's-land between the two enormous fleets, broadcasting a message on human battle frequencies – a message coded Priority Ten.

Benevenuto clenched his fists. What was happening now? In the entire history of the Empire there had only been seven Priority Ten alerts, signalling armed attack or rebellion. But he *knew* there was an armed attack here, that was what this whole situation was about; he didn't need someone to tell him the obvious.

Still, a Priority Ten call could not easily be ignored. Irritably he commanded that the message be broadcast directly to him. 'What is it?' he asked as the face of a stranger appeared on his small personal triscreen.

'Lady A's forces will betray you,' the man said. 'They'll catch you in a crossfire between themselves and the aliens.'

If this information was true, it would be very serious –

but Benevenuto couldn't just take the word of anyone who happened along in the middle of a battle. Not for something this crucial. 'What is the source of your information?' he asked.

'SOTE Agent Wombat,' Jules replied.

If Benevenuto had been a member of SOTE instead of a naval officer, he'd have believed what he heard implicitly. But the codename Wombat did not have the same legendary qualities in the Navy that it did in SOTE. Besides, he'd heard in all the briefings that Wombat had been killed on Omicron.

There was one way to resolve the problem quickly. Calling Captain Fortier to his side, he asked his aide to verify the identity of the caller. Fortier's eyes widened as he saw the face on the screen.

'Captain, please impress on the admiral the urgency of my information,' Jules said. 'I ended up behind alien lines, and I learned that there *are* no aliens – they're all robots manufactured by Lady A to fool us into this action. Once the battle begins, her ships will turn on you and pick you to pieces.'

Fortier did not hesitate. Turning quickly to his superior, he said, 'Sir, I urge you most strongly to listen to this advice. The source is unimpeachable.'

Fortunately for the Empire, Lord Admiral Benevenuto was mentally flexible enough to cope with so drastically changed a situation. Instead of having a unified force facing another smaller force, he was suddenly in a position of having a large enemy contingent in front of him and another large contingent scattered among his own ships. He immediately began issuing orders to fire on the conspiracy's ships, while the 'Gastaadi' ships were still out of range and unable to interfere.

The enemy forces did not remain idle. Lady A, in her own flagship, had also intercepted Jules's message, and knew instantly it could spell the end of her plans. It took a few minutes for many of the Navy's commanders to realize the change demanded of them and that they were at war with their supposed allies as well as with the aliens. The conspiracy's ships were under no such handicap; they'd been expecting all along to fire at the Navy ships, and were prepared when the order came to commence fighting.

At first the scene was total chaos as, from within the middle of the formation, conspiracy vessels fired at nearby Navy ships. The Empire lost almost fifty ships in that opening salvo before its crews could reorient their shields and turn their craft around to face the internal enemy. Undaunted by these initial losses, the Navy vessels engaged their foe, whom they outnumbered three-to-one, and began battling back.

The conflict was not that simple, though, as the pretended Gastaadi fleet flew into action. They swarmed toward the front lines of the Empire's formation and flew around to engage in a minor englobement. The Navy soon found itself fighting a battle on two different fronts against evenly matched opposition. Strategy was quickly thrown to the winds as the situation devolved to 'every ship for itself.' The outcome would now depend on the abilities and determination of the individual combatants.

The instant the attack orders were given and the battle began, Lady A's flagship tried to flee the scene. It broke from its assigned position and headed away from the fighting, out into open space. Its obvious intent was to reach a high enough speed to permit the jump into subspace, at which point it could escape to anywhere in the Galaxy. Captain Fortier, though, had been keeping a special eye on that ship, and the instant he saw it break formation he gave orders for a squadron of Navy ships to pursue and englobe. Lady A would not escape this time if he could help it.

Lady A's ship fired furiously at its pursuers, but the Navy vessels came on with dogged determination, englobing the bigger enemy flagship just out of its effective blaster range. Lady A's ship did not slow down, however, and the globe had to move with it if the ships in its forward line of motion were to avoid being shot. Fortier had to convince Lady A to stop before she reached subspace velocity and escaped his clutches.

Fortier opened a radio channel to the enemy leader. 'Stop or be destroyed,' he commanded.

The signal that came back was audio only, but he could easily imagine the sneer on Lady A's coldly beautiful face as she spoke. 'Do you really think it's that simple, Captain? You can blow my ship apart, and me with it, but you won't stop the conspiracy because the conspiracy *is* the Empire. That's the irony, Captain, and I hope you appreciate a good joke. You'll have to destroy the Empire in order to save it.'

The enemy flagship was almost up to subspace velocity. Sweat beaded on Fortier's forehead. He would have loved to capture Lady A alive, but if he waited a couple minutes more she'd be gone, and he might never have another chance. He could not be responsible for letting the most dangerous person in the Galaxy escape justice one more time. 'All ships, converge and fire,' he ordered the squadron that had englobed the flagship.

As it was, they were almost too late. The Navy vessels came in with their guns beaming rays at maximum intensity just as the enemy ship reached subspace velocity. Fortier drew in his breath, waiting. Then one of the rays struck the escaping craft squarely on the side, knocking enough power out of its shields that other rays could hit the ship and do their own damage. Before the flagship could drop into subspace, the deadly rays had penetrated its hull and knocked out the power systems. The ship was still flying through space at high speed, but it could no longer accelerate and it no longer had the power to drop into subspace.

'Prepare to board and capture,' Fortier ordered, but before his ships could obey there was a massive explosion like a supernova, and the flagship blew itself into flaming fragments that went hurtling through space at enormous speed. Lady A had suicided rather than be captured. Nothing could have survived that explosion, and his sensors verified his instincts. All that was left of the flagship and its crew was a mass of flying debris being scattered randomly to all ends of the universe. Nothing remained of the traitor or her crew.

Fortier let out a long sigh and ordered the squadron back into the battle. The leading figure of the conspiracy was gone, but that would make little difference in the long run if the Navy was defeated here.

If the enemy fleet was demoralized by the death of its leader, the effect hardly showed. The battle in this empty field of space lasted another fourteen hours as both sides fought with strength and resolve to break the other's spirit. Hundreds of ships on both sides of the conflict were destroyed and left to float in space – empty, airless hulks, a tribute to humanity's most destructive impulses. The largest battle ever waged became a graveyard of ships that would take many years to clean up again.

But eventually the forces fighting to protect their homes and loved ones proved to be made of sterner stuff than those fighting merely for power and money. There was no specific turning point, no time during the battle when the tide dramatically shifted in favor of the Empire. It was just that, after so many hours of continuous fighting, the enemy commanders looked around them and realized they were being outfought and gradually outnumbered. One by one, on the basis of individual decisions rather than conscious strategy, they tried to disengage and slip away from the fighting. Very few of them made it; those that did usually ended up as pirates within the Empire, to be rounded up at some later time by the Imperial Navy.

At last the conspiracy was left with just a small kernel of its once-mighty fleet. Realizing the war was lost the enemy leader, Admiral Shen, ordered retreat. He managed to escape with just a few hundred ships intact, to go off and lick their wounds and know that, without Lady A to lead them, their dreams of imperial conquest were probably over.

As for the Navy, its people were too tired and warmly happy to give much chase to the departing traitors. Twice in the past two years they had been severely tested and both times they had met the challenge. Their feeling of triumph was tempered by the knowledge that they had lost many gallant comrades in today's fighting; in all, more than a third of the Navy's total fleet was destroyed in the battle. But they had produced a feeling of security; after being stung so badly twice, no enemy would dare challenge the military might of the Empire for decades to come.

Lord Admiral Benevenuto gave the orders for the fleet to disperse. He looked forward to returning to his comfortable home on Luna Base and an end to all this bloodshed.

# CHAPTER 16

## 'The Conspiracy Is the Empire'

After delivering his vital warning, Jules d'Alembert found himself in a very awkward position. He was piloting a small, unarmed freighter right between two fleets about to engage in all-out war. He quickly decided he'd done all he could here; the presence or absence of his ship would make no difference in the outcome of the battle. It was prudence, not cowardice, that caused him to leave the scene; he realized he could serve the Empire better if he wasn't senselessly killed in a naval crossfire.

So, after seeing that his advice was followed, he turned his ship through a ninety-degree turn and sped away, dropping into subspace as soon as he'd reached proper velocity. He plotted in a course for Earth and leaned back in his couch to rest and arrange his thoughts. He would have a long and complex report to make when he returned to Headquarters.

His arrival back on Earth was a cause for great celebration by the friends who'd thought he was dead. After assuring them he was very much alive and giving the Head a brief synopsis of what he'd learned at the enemy base, he had a Service doctor examine his leg and bandage it securely for the first time since the injury. The bad news was that all the exertion while it was improperly treated may have permanently damaged some of the muscle tissue. It would be fine for normal use, even under heavy gravity conditions, but it might not hold up under the athletic activities he was accustomed to giving it.

Jules took the news philosophically. While he was disappointed, he and Yvette had known their days as

SOTE's prime agents were numbered, anyway. At this point, just being alive was a happy enough condition; anything else could sort itself out later.

He returned from the examination to the Head's office to find Helena and Yvette also there, waiting for him. After greeting them both with affectionate hugs and kisses, he proceeded to give them all a full rundown on everything that happened after Yvette saw him 'die' on Omicron. The Head made notes as Jules told him about the asteroid base and manufacturing plant, and everyone was silent as Jules related what he'd learned of Lady A's plans.

To cheer them up, the Head gave them the news of the fleet's victory over the enemy, which had just come in via subcom. Along with that came a report that Lady A had been destroyed while trying to escape. The group took that news with mixed emotions; while they were glad to be rid of their number one enemy, they regretted not being able to interrogate her on the details of her organization. They were also a little sorry they weren't able to prolong her punishment after all the misery she'd brought to the Empire – and particularly to Omicron. And, as Yvette commented, 'I'd still like to see the corpse for myself. That woman has more lives than a naughty Hindu.'

After giving his report, Jules went off to dinner with Yvette and Helena to celebrate his resurrection, while the Head stayed behind to put new plans into action. At dinner, Yvette admitted to being greatly relieved at seeing her brother alive again. 'I'm not just happy to have you back, but I really didn't know what to tell Vonnie. I hadn't called her yet to give her the bad news; now I don't have to.'

'Only too glad to spare you the inconvenience,' Jules said with a grin.

Things began happening very quickly at that point.

With the Navy no longer needed to guard the home worlds against a supposed alien invasion, a squadron of Imperial Marines was dispatched to take over Space Base 4. When they arrived at the coordinates Jules gave, however, they found nothing there but a rapidly expanding cloud of debris. Rather than let the Empire discover anything further about their plans, the conspiracy had destroyed the base. No one could ever be sure whether the people aboard it had been evacuated or whether they'd been sacrificed for the sake of expediency.

The woman Tatiana, whose real name was Inge Durmweiler, was questioned under detrazine regarding her role in the Omicron affair. She turned out to have no knowledge of the hoax, nor of the conspiracy in general. She was just a linguistics scholar whose education had been sponsored by Lady A in return for some favors, and she'd honestly thought she was evaluating the language of an alien culture. Since she had no previous criminal record and no serious connections to the conspiracy she was given an imperial pardon and allowed to return to her studies, with the warning that her activities would be closely monitored by SOTE and she would not be given the chance to work on any security-sensitive projects. She accepted those conditions gladly, and went on to lead an exemplary life.

At the same time the Imperial Marines were sent to Space Base 4, an expedition was dispatched to Omicron to remove any 'aliens' who might still be enslaving the people. Once again they found they were too late; the enemy had already pulled back, taking all its forces off the planet and leaving the citizens bewildered and frightened, wondering what this horror had been all about.

As soon as the world was declared safe, Edna Stanley traveled all the way to Omicron on a personal inspection tour, making her the first reigning monarch in history to travel that far from the seat of government. She visited the bombed-out cities and spoke to the small clusters of people who'd begun making their way from their hiding places in the country back into the civilized world again. The Empress promised unlimited disaster relief aid to all of Omicron and pledged that what had happened here would be remembered by the entire Galaxy. A special memorial to the millions who had died would be built in Moscow, and great care would be taken to ensure that nothing like this would ever happen again.

The Omicronians responded with overwhelming enthusiasm and a great outpouring of love for their Empress – and as the news reports of what had happened filtered through the rest of the Galaxy the sentiments were repeated on every human-occupied planet. In just two short years, Empress Stanley Eleven had managed to make herself as loved and respected as her father had before her.

While the Empress was on her way back to Earth, Helena von Wilmenhorst gave a small, intimate dinner party. Her guests were her father, Jules and Yvette, and of course Captain Paul Fortier, freshly returned with the admiral's flagship. There the official announcement of the engagement was made, amid great cheers and general happiness. Jules announced he'd be leaving soon for Nereid to retrieve *La Comète Cuivré*, and Yvette said she'd be returning to DesPlaines by herself; she'd been away from Pias and little Kari far too long. After a fine dinner and many rounds of toasts, however, the conversation turned to business once more.

'What I'd like to know,' Yvette said, sipping her orange juice slowly, 'is, if the aliens were a hoax, where did their strange technology come from? How did they manage to jam all the subcom signals to and from Omicron after their invasion, and particularly . . .'

She paused and shuddered, remembering her horrifying experience at the slave camp. 'Particularly, how did they come up with that controlling ray? We don't have anything like that.'

The Head frowned. 'This has worried me the past few days, myself. Of course, the conspiracy has its own advanced technology research, Dr Loxner being a prime example. Pirates have been jamming the subcom transmissions of their victims for years, and the Navy's been working on a wide-spectrum jammer off and on, with mixed success. Some of the data may actually have been stolen from our own research labs. We're looking into that possibility.

'And as for the controlling ray, you're wrong – we do have something like it: nitrobarb.'

'But that's a drug, not a ray,' Yvette objected.

'It wasn't the ray alone that did the job,' the Grand Duke explained. 'The collar you wore contained a tiny hyposprayer and a mild nitrobarb derivative, while the ray was a very weak stun. The ray did two things. First, it stopped you in your tracks without knocking you unconscious – and second, it caused the collar to inject you with the drug, which quickly sapped your will like nitrobarb does – without, luckily, the lethal side effects.

'It took both the ray and the collar to produce that illusion, which is why the aliens couldn't use that weapon against the freedom fighters in the cities – they hadn't been banded yet. Lady A wanted to convince us there was a truly alien force there, so she made things seem as unusual as she could – but the enemy doesn't have anything yet that will enslave you from a distance.'

'That's a relief,' Yvette said.

'What bothers me is how we were so badly fooled,' Fortier complained. 'It makes me feel like a prize idiot.'

'You're nothing of the kind,' Helena said, leaping to

her fiancé's defense. 'You weren't fooled at all. There really *was* an invasion by nonhuman creatures. Lady A knew you were all too good to be taken in by a fake, which was why the takeover had to be so thorough; nothing less would have worked. She simply came along to make sure you didn't find out too much about the nature of the invaders. The situation you were in was *very* real, and she let it kill one of her own people to add a convincing touch.'

'Every time we've had our eyes opened about her and thought she couldn't fool us again, she always found another twist,' Jules said. 'I don't think I'm going to miss her much.'

'But what about the conspiracy now that she's gone?' Yvette mused. 'We still don't have a single clue about the identity of C – if he does in fact exist. They've still got a large organization, a few hundred ships, and at least eight more of those space bases. Even after a rattlesnake is dead, its fangs still have enough poison to kill you.'

'I can't forget what she said, that the conspiracy *is* the Empire,' Fortier said. 'That's an exact quote. She said it was a joke, an irony, that we'd have to destroy the Empire in order to save it.'

The five of them sat silently around the table contemplating those remarks. Finally Helena spoke up. 'Well, I think she was just being vicious. That was just like her. She knew she was going to die and she wanted to spoil our victory. She wanted one last chance to spit in our faces. I don't think it means anything.'

At this point Zander von Wilmenhorst changed the subject back to the original reason for the dinner, Helena's engagement. There were many practical considerations to be dealt with. As a duchess and heir to one of the richest Sectors of the Galaxy, her marriage would be a formal court affair, and would require months of preparation. The five friends quickly lost themselves in a sea of logistical details that made military maneuvers seem trivial by comparison.

But after leaving his daughter's apartment, von Wilmenhorst returned to his office high in the Hall of State for Sector Four. He left the room dark and opened the curtains, gazing idly down along the eastern Florida coastline. The night was moonless and rainy, adding a grim touch to his already melancholy mood.

Lady A was not a woman given to idle gestures or statements. She often lied – but the best lies always included enough truth to give them bite. Her parting declaration worried him, and he kept turning it over in his mind.

'The conspiracy *is* the Empire.' Much as he wanted to dismiss it as Helena had, all his instincts told him there was a vital bit of meat hidden under that large nutshell. He could almost hear Lady A's mocking laugh taunting him as he tried without success to unravel her final riddle, 'You'll have to destroy the Empire in order to save it.' He could not avoid the feeling that the security of the Empire was bound up in those simple words.

With a sigh, Zander von Wilmenhorst closed the curtains, turned on the lights and returned to the everpresent stack of papers on his desk. There was work to be done.

# The world's greatest science fiction authors now available in Panther Books

**E E 'Doc' Smith**

*The Classic 'Lensman' series*

| | | |
|---|---|---|
| Masters of the Vortex | £1.50 | ☐ |
| Children of the Lens | £1.95 | ☐ |
| Second Stage Lensman | £1.25 | ☐ |
| Grey Lensman | £1.95 | ☐ |
| Galactic Patrol | £1.50 | ☐ |
| First Lensman | £1.25 | ☐ |
| Triplanetary | £1.50 | ☐ |

*The 'Skylark' series*

| | | |
|---|---|---|
| The Skylark of Space | £1.25 | ☐ |
| Skylark Three | £1.25 | ☐ |
| The Skylark of Valeron | £1.50 | ☐ |
| Skylark Duquesne | £1.25 | ☐ |

*The 'Family D'Alembert' series* (with Stephen Goldin)

| | | |
|---|---|---|
| The Imperial Stars | £1.25 | ☐ |
| Stranglers' Moon | £1.25 | ☐ |
| The Clockwork Traitor | £1.95 | ☐ |
| Getaway World | £1.25 | ☐ |
| The Bloodstar Conspiracy | £1.50 | ☐ |
| The Purity Plot | £1.25 | ☐ |
| Planet of Treachery | £1.25 | ☐ |
| Eclipsing Binaries | £1.50 | ☐ |

*Other Titles*

| | | |
|---|---|---|
| Subspace Explorers | £1.25 | ☐ |
| The Galaxy Primes | £1.50 | ☐ |
| Spacehounds of IPC | £1.25 | ☐ |

To order direct from the publisher just tick the titles you want and fill in the order form.

All these books are available at your local bookshop or newsagent, or can be ordered direct from the publisher.

*To order direct from the publisher just tick the titles you want and fill in the form below.*

**Name** _____

**Address** _____

_____

Send to:
**Panther Cash Sales**
**PO Box 11, Falmouth, Cornwall TR10 9EN.**

Please enclose remittance to the value of the cover price plus:

**UK** 45p for the first book, 20p for the second book plus 14p per copy for each additional book ordered to a maximum charge of £1.63.

**BFPO and Eire** 45p for the first book, 20p for the second book plus 14p per copy for the next 7 books, thereafter 8p per book.

**Overseas** 75p for the first book and 21p for each additional book.

Panther Books reserve the right to show new retail prices on covers, which may differ from those previously advertised in the text or elsewhere.